Pegasus Princesses
FLIP'S FAIR

Emily Bliss
illustrated by Sydney Hanson

BLOOMSBURY
CHILDREN'S BOOKS
NEW YORK LONDON OXFORD NEW DELHI SYDNEY

BLOOMSBURY CHILDREN'S BOOKS
Bloomsbury Publishing Inc., part of Bloomsbury Publishing Plc
1385 Broadway, New York, NY 10018

BLOOMSBURY, BLOOMSBURY CHILDREN'S BOOKS, and the Diana logo
are trademarks of Bloomsbury Publishing Plc

First published in the United States of America in March 2022
by Bloomsbury Children's Books

Bloomsbury books may be purchased for business or promotional use. For information on bulk
purchases please contact Macmillan Corporate and Premium Sales Department at
specialmarkets@macmillan.com

Library of Congress Cataloging-in-Publication Data
Names: Bliss, Emily, author. | Hanson, Sydney, illustrator.
Title: Flip's fair / by Emily Bliss ; illustrated by Sydney Hanson.
Description: New York : Bloomsbury Children's Books, 2022. | Series: Pegasus princesses ;
3 Audience: Ages 7–10 | Audience: Grades 2–3
Summary: Princess Flip and her sisters have invented the perfect potion to bring to the
Wing Realm's annual potion fair, but when a potion mishap causes a caterpillar catastrophe, the
Pegasus princesses will need all of Clara's creativity to save the day!—provided by publisher.
Identifiers: LCCN 2021042536 (print) | LCCN 2021042537 (e-book)
ISBN 978-1-5476-0837-9 (paperback) • ISBN 978-1-5476-0839-3 (e-book)
Subjects: CYAC: Winged horses—Fiction. | Princesses—Fiction. | Magic—Fiction. |
Imaginary creatures—Fiction. | LCGFT: Novels.
Classification: LCC PZ7.1.B633 Fli 2022 (print) | LCC PZ7.1.B633 (e-book) | DDC [Fic]—dc23
LC record available at https://lccn.loc.gov/2021042536
LC e-book record available at https://lccn.loc.gov/2021042537

Book design by John Candell
Typeset by Westchester Publishing Services
Printed in the U.S.A.
2 4 6 8 10 9 7 5 3 1

To find out more about our authors and books visit www.bloomsbury.com
and sign up for our newsletters.

For Phoenix and Lynx

Pegasus Princesses

FLIP'S FAIR

Chapter One

On a sunny Saturday afternoon, Clara Griffin and her younger sister, Miranda, crouched by the creek behind their house. Between the girls, nestled in the muddy creek bank, sat a metal bucket filled with water, shredded leaves, moss, sand, mud, acorns, pebbles, and crushed pine cones.

"The potion definitely needs another

handful of pegasus laughter," Clara said. She reached into the creek and grabbed a fistful of mud from the bottom. Tiny rivers of dirty water ran down her arm as she dropped the mud into the bucket with a giant splash. Clara giggled as potion splattered all over her T-shirt and shorts—and all over Miranda's blue raincoat, blue rain pants, and blue rain boots.

"Clara!" Miranda said in a voice that was half-annoyed and half-amused. Unlike Clara, Miranda did not usually like getting muddy or wet.

"Oops," Clara said. "Sorry about that."

"It's okay," Miranda said, smiling and shrugging. "It's a good thing I put on my rain gear. Anyway, the potion needs more

stardust." She turned to a patch of dry sand and grabbed a handful. She held her hand over the bucket and opened her fingers so slowly that the sand slid into the potion without splashing at all.

"Now we need to stir it," Clara said. She stood up, skipped over to a pine tree, and found two sticks on the forest floor. She skipped back to Miranda and handed her one. "These can be our spoons," Clara suggested.

"Good idea," Miranda said.

Clara kneeled next to the pot so her knees sank right into the mud. She pushed her stick into the thick potion. But when she tried to stir, the stick snapped in two.

"Maybe this one will work better,"

Miranda said, but her stick also broke as soon as she tried to stir with it.

"I know," Clara said, standing up. "I'll go get spoons from the kitchen."

"Dad said we couldn't take any of the spoons in the silverware drawer out to the creek," Miranda said.

"Oh yeah," Clara said, her shoulders sinking. "I forgot."

The two sisters were silent for a few seconds. And then Clara remembered she had an old purple ruler in her room—maybe it would work for stirring potion! "I know what we can use," she said, jumping up and down.

Miranda smiled. "You look like an excited kangaroo," she said.

Clara giggled. "I'll be right back," she said, sprinting in the direction of their house.

"Make sure you use the hose to wash off before you go inside," Miranda called after her.

Clara rolled her eyes. But she also knew her sister was right. Her parents would not like it if she ran through the house covered in mud. When she got to her yard, she ran around to the side of her family's stone house and turned the blue metal spigot connected to the green garden hose. Soon, water gushed from the hose nozzle. Clara—pretending she was an elephant and the hose was her trunk—sprayed water all over herself until she was dripping wet but clean.

Clara skipped to the back of her house and slid her feet out of her flip-flops, which were still a little muddy. She opened the screen door and ran barefoot into her kitchen. She was relieved to notice neither of her parents was there to tell her she was too wet to be running through the house. Clara dashed across her kitchen and through her living room. She bounded up the stairs two at a time. She galloped down the hall. And she burst into her bedroom.

Clara tried to remember where she had left her ruler. Recently, it had been a drumstick, a slide for her plastic tyrannosaurus family, and a tabletop for a stuffed hedge-hog. But she was pretty sure the ruler was now a seesaw for two baby merfairies—mermaids with wings. Clara leaped over a unicorn ski slope she had built out of balls of crumpled purple and pink paper. She crawled through a fort she had constructed from four chairs and all the sheets and tow-els she could find in the linen closet. She slid around a pegasus sculpture made out of cardboard boxes, milk jugs, pipe clean-ers, tin foil, and braided yarn. And then she spotted the ruler on her bureau, bal-anced on top of an unopened can of tuna. Sure enough, a baby merfairy, sculpted out of modeling clay, sat on each end. Clara opened one of her bureau drawers and gently nestled the baby merfairies between two folded T-shirts. "Have a nice nap," she whispered to them, leaving the drawer open so they wouldn't feel scared. She picked up the ruler and was just about to sprint out of the house and back to Miranda when she heard a humming noise coming from under her bed.

Clara froze. The humming noise grew louder. She listened to it for a few seconds, and then she grinned from ear to ear. She hopped over to her bed, kneeled, and pulled out a shoebox she had decorated with sequins, glitter, and paint. She flipped open the lid, and there inside the box was only one thing: a silver feather. Light shot up and down the feather's spine as it hummed louder and louder.

Clara sucked in her breath. The feather had been a special gift from the pegasus princesses—eight royal pegasus sisters who lived with their pet cat, Lucinda, in a magical world called the Wing Realm. Each pegasus had a unique power and a special, magical tiara. Silver Princess Mist could turn invisible. Teal Princess Aqua could breathe underwater and make magic bubbles. Peach Princess Flip could do a special somersault and turn into any animal. Black Princess Star had extraordinary senses. Pink Princess Rosie could speak and understand any language. White Princess Snow could freeze things and make winter weather. Green Princess Stitch could sew, knit, and crochet anything. And lavender Princess Dash could magically transport herself anywhere in the Wing Realm in an instant.

Whenever the pegasus princesses wanted to invite Clara to Feather Palace, the wing-shaped castle they called home, they made the silver feather shimmer and hum— just the way it was shimmering and humming right then! To get to the Wing Realm, all Clara had to do was hold the feather in her hands as she ran to a special place by a large pine tree in the woods surrounding her house.

Clara picked up the feather. She crawled back through the fort and leaped over the ski slope. She was halfway through her bedroom doorway when she noticed her soaking wet clothes and her bare feet. As much as Clara enjoyed getting wet and being barefoot, she wanted dry clothes and sneakers for her next adventure in the Wing Realm.

Clara set down the feather and ruler on floor next to her door. She peeled off her shorts and T-shirt and threw them into her green hamper. Then she surveyed her room for clothes to put on. Her favorite rainbow-striped tights hung from her ceiling fan to make a swing for her stuffed caterpillar. She climbed onto her bed, pulled down the tights, untied the knot she'd made with the feet, and put them on. She spotted a peach-colored skirt and a butterfly T-shirt on her bedside table, where she had used them, along with some popsicle sticks, to make a camping tent for her pegasus figures. Clara slid the skirt on over her legs and pulled the T-shirt over her head. Finally, she found her favorite

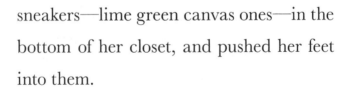

sneakers—lime green canvas ones—in the bottom of her closet, and pushed her feet into them.

She danced back over to her bedroom door and picked up the feather and the ruler. She hid the feather in her skirt pocket and raced out of her bedroom, along the hall, down the stairs, through the living room, across the kitchen, and out the backdoor.

Clara sprinted across her yard, into the woods, and back to the place by the creek where Miranda was adding daisy petals to their potion.

"Try this," Clara said, out of breath and smiling as she handed the ruler to her sister. "I need to go do something really fast and then I'll be back to keep playing." Time in the human world froze while Clara was in the Wing Realm, meaning that even if she stayed with the pegasus princesses for hours, Miranda would think she had been gone for only a minute or two.

"Thanks," Miranda said. She pushed the ruler into the potion and tried to stir. The ruler began to bend. "I think it's about to break," she said.

Clara nodded. "I think you're right. Why don't you add some unicorn snort and mermaid singing while I'm gone? I'll try to bring back something else to use to stir," she said.

Miranda nodded. "See you in a minute," she said.

Clara leaped across the creek and ran along it until she was out of Miranda's sight. She pulled the feather out of her pocket as she turned left, jogging deeper into the woods. She ran down a hill, through a grove of pine trees, and into a small clearing. Pine needles covered the ground, and a large pine tree with green boughs stood opposite her. She took a step closer to the pine tree. In a swirl of glittery light, a green velvet armchair with silver-feathered wings on its back appeared. The armchair hopped up and down and then spun in a circle on one of its legs. Clara giggled. The armchair bounded over to her. It leaned toward her and nudged her—almost, Clara thought, like a friendly dog wanting attention.

"Hello, chair," Clara said, laughing.

The chair fluttered its wings.

"Will you take me to Feather Palace?" she asked.

The chair hopped up and down.

"Wonderful," Clara said. She slid the feather back into her pocket. She sat down on the chair and grabbed its arms.

The chair flapped its wings and leaped upward. It landed for a few seconds on a tree branch, bounced for a moment on the bough, and then soared into the air. The chair skidded onto the tile roof of Clara's house and then beat its wings as it flew upward. The chair began to spin, faster and faster, as it rocketed into the clouds. Clara sucked in her breath as everything went pitch black. And then the chair landed with a clatter on a tile floor.

Chapter Two

Clara blinked and opened her eyes. She knew exactly where she was: the front hall of Feather Palace. Portraits of the eight pegasus princesses and Lucinda hung on the magenta walls. Fountains with pegasus sculptures spouted rainbow-colored water. Pegasus statues reared up with outstretched wings from pedestals. Gauzy curtains fluttered as a warm breeze blew through the tall windows. Light from the chandeliers shimmered and danced on the black tile floors. In the center of the room, the pegasus princesses' eight empty thrones formed a half-circle. Next to Flip's peach throne sat a small silver sofa with a back that looked like a cat head. And on the sofa perched Lucinda, who was so absorbed in licking her hind foot that she didn't even notice Clara.

Clara stood up. Lucinda kept licking her foot. Clara cleared her throat. Lucinda moved on to cleaning the tip of her tail. Finally, in a soft voice, Clara said, "Hello there."

Lucinda leaped up into the air and hovered above her sofa. For a split second, she looked at Clara with wide, startled, green eyes. Then she let out a loud purring noise and flew straight over to Clara. The tip of Lucinda's nose touched the tip of Clara's nose as the cat purred, "I've been waiting and waiting and waiting for you. Welcome back to Feather Palace."

"I'm thrilled to be here," Clara said, scratching behind Lucinda's ears.

"Princess Flip told me to call her the instant you arrived. She told me absolutely no guessing games because they take too long. But," Lucinda continued, "I'm sure there's time for just one. Don't you think?"

Clara laughed. She had never met anyone who loved guessing games as much as Lucinda.

Still hovering in front of Clara's face, Lucinda flipped onto her back with her paws sticking straight up into the air. "How about if *you* guess this time?" she suggested, swishing her tail.

"Okay," Clara said, surprised. Usually Lucinda liked to do the guessing.

"I'll think of an easy one. How about," Lucinda said slowly, "if you guess my middle name? I'll give you three tries."

Clara didn't think that sounded easy at all. "Okay," she said. "Would you be willing to give me a hint?"

"Absolutely not," Lucinda said.

"Um," Clara said, thinking of names of kids in her class. "Is it Renee?"

"Nope," Lucinda said, righting herself

and flying over to Clara's shoulder, where she perched and purred. Clara smiled at the feeling of Lucinda's soft fur on her cheek.

"How about Tolonda?" Clara guessed.

"Wrong again," Lucinda said, swooping down to the floor and rubbing against Clara's ankles.

"Um. Is it Kira?" Clara asked.

"Wrong again," Lucinda said. She puffed up her chest, held her head high, and announced, "It's Mariettatonya. My full name is Lucinda Mariettatonya Salisbury-Heffenhopper the Third."

Clara giggled. "That's a wonderful name," she said.

"Thank you," Lucinda said. "And now I

think I better call Princess Flip." She bounded to the center of the front hall and called out, "Princess Flip! Clara got here this very second! We definitely did not play any guessing games! Not even one!"

After a few seconds, Clara heard the clatter of hooves against the palace's tile floors. The sound grew louder and louder. And then Flip galloped into the front hall wearing goggles and a pointy peach wizard's hat with a silver spiral design that matched the gemstone pattern on her tiara. "I'm so glad you're here!" Flip exclaimed, rearing up with excitement. "You've arrived just in time. Welcome back to the Wing Realm."

"Thank you for inviting me," Clara said.

Flip looked at Lucinda. The pegasus cocked her head and smiled. "Are you sure you didn't play any guessing games?" she asked. "Not even one?"

Lucinda sniffed and twitched her tail. "Well, maybe one," she admitted before sauntering over to her cat sofa and curling up in a ball. "Don't mind me," she said between yawns. "I'm due for my morning nap. Her eyelids fluttered and then shut. She let out a loud noise that was half-purr and half-snore.

Clara giggled. Flip shook her head in amusement before she turned to Clara. "I can't wait to tell you what we're doing this afternoon. It's my favorite day of the year.

Today is our annual Potion Fair. Teams of creatures from all over the Wing Realm spend the year inventing and perfecting new magic potions. Then we bring them to the fair and share them with each other. Would you like to join us?"

"I would love to join you," Clara said.

"I'm so glad," Flip said. "Especially since this year my sisters and I invented a potion with you in mind."

"Really?" Clara asked.

"Really," Flip said, eyes gleaming. "We invented a flying potion. If you sprinkle it over your head, you'll be able to fly even though you don't have wings."

"That sounds amazing," Clara said.

"You can try it as soon as we finish mixing the final batch. Want to come down to Feather Palace's potion laboratory to help us?"

"I'd love to," Clara said.

"Follow me," Flip said. She reared up and whinnied with delight before she trotted across the front hall and down a narrow corridor with black tile floors and lanterns that burned rainbow flames. Clara followed Flip to the end of the corridor and down three flights of a spiral staircase. At the bottom, they came to two wooden double doors carved with pictures of feather-winged cauldrons. Above the doors, a sign read, "Feather Laboratory."

Flip pushed the doors open with her nose, and she and Clara stepped into a laboratory the size of Clara's living room. A chandelier made of small silver cauldrons hung from the ceiling. Tall shelves crammed with glass jars, each full of a powder or liquid, lined all four walls. In one corner, towers of stacked cauldrons teetered. In another corner, a giant rack held empty glass potion bottles. In the center of the laboratory, the seven other pegasus princesses gathered around a giant, shiny, peach-colored cauldron. They all wore goggles and pointy wizard's hats. And they all held purple mixing spoons in their mouths.

As soon as Mist, Aqua, Star, Snow,

Rosie, Dash, and Stitch saw Clara, they dropped their spoons into the cauldron and galloped over to her.

"Clara!" Mist called out. "You made it!"

"Welcome back, human friend," Aqua said, dancing in a circle around Clara.

"We are so pleased you're here," Star said, swishing her tail.

Rosie playfully poked Clara's arm with the tip of her bright pink pointy hat.

Snow and Dash reared up, grinned, and flapped their wings so their hooves lifted off the floor.

"Guess what?" Stitch said. "I have a surprise for you." She galloped across the room to a large bag made of glittery green fabric. Stitch picked up the bag with her mouth, galloped over to Clara, and dropped the bag into Clara's hands. "I can't wait for you to open it," Stitch said.

Clara sucked in her breath. She stuck her hand into the bag and pulled out a pointy green velvet hat and a pair of goggles.

"Those are for you," Stitch said.

"Thank you so much," Clara said.

"You're welcome," Stitch said with a wink. "I used my favorite fabric to sew your hat. And I borrowed those goggles from our fairy friends. They're fairy size extra-extra-extra-large. Hopefully they'll fit a human girl."

Clara put on the goggles and the hat.

"These fit perfectly," she said, grinning. She twirled in a circle. "How do I look?" she asked.

"Ready to make a potion," Flip said, laughing.

"Come on over to the cauldron," Mist said.

Clara and the eight pegasus princesses huddled around the cauldron. Clara peered down to see a bubbling scarlet potion.

"We've already added dehydrated dragon fire, phoenix song, merfairy humming, pink mist, and shredded rainbow seaweed," Flip explained.

"Because we have hooves instead of hands, two fairies helped us open the jars and put in the ingredients," Aqua said.

"But they left so they could go finish making their own potion for the fair," Mist said.

"So," Flip said hopefully, "we were wondering if you would help us add the last three ingredients."

"Absolutely," Clara said.

"The next ingredient we need is one pinch of snail trail. The potion ingredients are arranged in ABC order," Flip explained. "So the snail trail should be in the S section."

Clara looked at the shelves. She noticed a card with a Q written on it taped to a shelf. She looked to the right and saw an R card. She looked further to the right until she saw a shelf with an S card on it. Clara

skipped over to it. She saw jars with labels that read SATURN RING DUST, SEA BREEZE, SILENT LAUGHTER, and STEW STEAM. Then, right between jars labeled SMILES and SNAKE SLITHER, was a jar full of silver dust labeled SNAIL TRAIL. Clara grabbed

the snail trail off the shelf and skipped over to the cauldron, where all eight pegasus princesses eagerly held their spoons in their mouths. Flip nodded encouragingly at Clara.

Clara removed the lid, pinched the dust with her fingers, and dropped it into the cauldron. As the potion bubbled and churned, the pegasus princesses stirred and stirred. After a few seconds, the potion had turned bright pumpkin orange.

Flip dropped her spoon. "That was perfect," she said. "Now we need one handful of butterfly flutter."

"One handful of butterfly flutter coming up," Clara said. She put the lid back on the snail trail and returned the jar to its place on the *S* shelves before she skipped across the laboratory to the *B* section.

Clara saw jars labeled, Bat Sleep, Bear Growls, and Bent Rainbows. And then, right between Bumblebee Buzz and Burst Balloons, was a tall jar of yellow powder labeled Butterfly Flutter. Clara picked it up and noticed it felt warm. She skipped back over to the cauldron, opened the jar, and grabbed a handful of what felt like sand that had been out in the summer sun. She dropped the butterfly flutter into the cauldron. The potion frothed as the pegasus princesses stirred it until it was lemon yellow.

Flip put down her spoon and said, "There's only one more ingredient—a splash of cat purr. But just be careful not to get the cat sneeze by accident."

Clara nodded. She put the jar of butterfly flutter back and found the shelves with *C* ingredients. She saw jars labeled CURLED DOG BARK, COBWEB SILK, and CHIPMUNK CHIRPS. Then she spotted a jar of glittery light-blue liquid labeled CAT PURR. It was right between jars with the labels CAT BLINK and CAT SNEEZE. Clara was careful to choose the cat purr. She skipped over to the cauldron and unscrewed the top. She tilted the jar to one side and flicked her wrist as though she were throwing a frisbee. Light blue liquid splashed out of the jar and into the cauldron. The potion bubbled and foamed. Clara screwed the lid back onto the jar and returned it to the shelves while the pegasus princesses stirred.

After several seconds, the potion stopped bubbling. It looked thick and lime green.

The pegasus princesses dropped their spoons into the cauldron. "It's finally ready," Flip said. She grinned at Clara. "Would you like to try it right now?"

"Yes," Clara said, jumping up and down.

Chapter Three

The pegasus princesses reared up and whinnied.

"I can't wait to see if it works," Dash said.

"I'm so excited I can hardly stand to watch," Snow said.

"All you need to do is reach into the cauldron and sprinkle some potion on the top of your head," Flip said.

"But maybe you should take off your hat and goggles first," Stitch said. "The potion only works if it touches your head."

Clara nodded. She took off her pointy hat and goggles and set them down on the floor. She dipped her hand into the potion, which felt like warm chocolate sauce. She scooped some up and splashed it onto her head. Clara smiled as the potion ran down her forehead, nose, and cheeks. Then, she opened her eyes to find that the pegasus princesses were all staring at her with wide, unblinking eyes.

"At least we know this version of the potion doesn't make you grow a tail," Aqua said. "That was the problem with the last one."

"Or horns," Mist added. "That was the problem with the version before that one."

"Or whiskers," Aqua said. "That was the problem with the first version we invented."

Flip smiled reassuringly at Clara. "Let's see if it works," she said. "What happens if you imagine you're flying up to the chandelier?"

Star and Rosie sucked in their breath.

Stitch crossed her hooves for good luck.

Dash bit her lip.

Snow anxiously swished her tail.

"Here goes," Clara said. She imagined she was shooting upward. To her amazement, her feet lifted right off the black tile floor, and in a half-second she was

hovering right next to the chandelier. She laughed with delight.

"It worked!" Stitch said, uncrossing her legs and rearing up.

"I can hardly believe it," Rosie said, shaking her head.

"Hooray!" cheered Aqua and Dash.

"You're a natural flyer!" Flip exclaimed.

"I'm so glad we made a double batch of this version," Star said.

"What a relief," Snow said.

Flip flapped her wings and joined Clara in the air. "Try flying around the chandelier," she suggested.

Clara imagined flying in a circle. She bolted forward and zoomed around the chandelier, barreling toward Flip.

"Whoa," Flip said, laughing and ducking to avoid a collision. "I think we'd better go outside before we crash into the shelves of potion ingredients and make a giant mess."

"My parents would definitely tell me flying is an outdoor activity," Clara said. She flew downward until her sneakers were back on the floor. Flip landed with a clatter next to her.

"And besides, it's about time for me to go to the Magic Marsh to make sure everything is ready for the Potion Fair," Flip said. "Would you like to fly along with me? I'd love to have your help."

"Yes," Clara said. Her heart quickened

at the thought of flying through the wide open sky, right next to Flip.

"Excellent," Flip said. She turned to Star. "Would you mind coming to the Magic Marsh a little early and bringing the potion with you? I don't want to bring it now just in case Clara needs some help flying."

"Of course," Star said. "And since we made a double batch, why don't I bring half of it to the fair and leave half of it here for the next time Clara visits?"

"Great idea," Flip said. "Thank you."

Clara turned toward the laboratory door, but then she noticed that the pegasus princesses were exchanging nervous looks.

She worried that she had grown a tail, horns, or whiskers after all.

"Um, there's just one more thing," Star said. "Though we're a little embarrassed to ask."

"Before you go—" Rosie began, and then she frowned.

"Is there any chance you could just—" Snow continued.

"Take off our hats and goggles for us?" Aqua finished.

"The fairies put them on us," Mist explained.

"And getting them off is just a little complicated with—" Dash said.

"Hooves," all eight pegasus princesses said at once.

Clara laughed. "Of course," she said. "I'd be glad to help."

She skipped over to Flip and pulled off her peach hat and goggles. Then she took off Star's black hat and goggles, Aqua's teal hat and goggles, Mist's silver hat and goggles, Dash's purple hat and goggles, Stitch's green hat and goggles, Rosie's pink hat and goggles, and Snow's white hat and goggles.

"Thank you," Flip said.

"And just one more thing," Star said. "Will you pour half of the flying potion into one of those empty cauldrons? I'm not so sure I can do it without spilling a lot of it."

"Life with hooves is really tricky," Aqua said, sighing and rolling her eyes.

"Of course I can help with that," Clara said. She pulled an empty peach-colored cauldron off the top of one of the stacks. She set it down next to the cauldron full of potion. Then she bent her knees, wrapped her arms around the full cauldron, and used all her strength to pick it up. She poured half the green potion into the empty cauldron. "Phew," Clara said, putting down the cauldron.

"Thank you so much," Star said.

"I promise we would want to be friends with

you even if you didn't have hands," Flip said.

"But I have to admit it's helpful that you have them," Snow said.

"It sure is handy that you have hands," Stitch said, rolling her eyes at her own bad joke.

Clara giggled.

"Let's fly to the Magic Marsh now," Flip said to Clara. She turned to Star and added, "I'll see you there in just a few minutes."

"The rest of us will join you there right before the Potion Fair," Aqua said.

"Wonderful," Flip said. She turned to Clara. "Follow me!"

Clara followed Flip out of the

laboratory, up the spiral staircase, and back into the front hall.

"Do you feel ready for your first trip through the sky?" Flip asked.

"I'm ready," Clara said, and she felt her heart quicken.

"And if anything goes wrong, I'll be right next to you," Flip said.

Clara nodded. "Thank you," she said.

"At the count of three, let's both run toward the front doors. One. Two. Three. Go!" Flip said.

Flip galloped and Clara sprinted across the front hall. The doors magically swung open to reveal an expanse of blue sky. Down below, Clara saw an ocean of green tree-tops. Flip leaped out, flapped her wings, and soared into the air. Clara sucked in her breath, took a giant jump out the doors, and imagined flying alongside Flip. The next thing she knew, she and Flip were flying side by side.

Chapter Four

Clara's heart raced as wind riffled through her wavy black hair. For a moment, she turned her head and looked back at Feather Palace. The silver, wing-shaped castle's towers and turrets shimmered in the sunlight. Clara faced forward, gazing at the expanse of blue sky below her and ahead of her.

"Flying is so much fun," Clara said.

"I had a feeling you'd like it," Flip said.

Clara made a fist and then raised her arm so she felt like a superhero. "I'm Super Clara!" she called out.

Flip raised one of her front legs and said, "And I'm Super Flip!"

Clara and Flip laughed.

Clara turned upside down and flew feet first. Flip turned upside down and flew hooves first.

Clara did a somersault in the air. Flip did a somersault next to her.

Flip's eyes widened and twinkled. "Somersaulting just made me think of a way we could have a little fun while we fly to the Magic Marsh. Do you ever like to play games where you pretend to be different animals?"

"All the time," Clara said, nodding. "My sister Miranda and I pretended to be wolves and cheetahs this morning before breakfast. And sometimes we're greyhounds, kittens, and bumblebees."

Flip flashed Clara an excited smile and said, "Watch this." The gemstone spiral design on her tiara glittered. She did a somersault. And then there was a large peach wolf with wings flying right next to Clara. Flip the wolf turned toward Clara and winked a glowing, amber eye. Then she raised her head and made a soft howling noise.

Clara giggled. She looked upward and howled back. "I'm a wolf, too," she said in a low, raspy voice. "Woof! Woof!"

"Sometimes if I howl loudly enough, real wolves howl back," Flip barked. "Want to try it?"

Clara glanced down to see that she and Flip were passing over a thick, dark pine forest. It looked like a perfect home for wolves. "Absolutely," she said. "Let's pretend we see the moon."

Clara and Flip both looked upward at an imaginary moon and made the loudest, shrillest howling noises they could for as long as they could. When they were out of breath, they stopped and listened. Soon

Clara heard high-pitched howling coming from the forest below.

Flip pricked up her wolf ears and grinned.

Clara grinned back.

Flip winked and somersaulted. In an instant, she was a pegasus again.

Clara glanced down and saw that the woods below had thinned into a giant meadow full of wild flowers. Flip followed her gaze. "That's where the butterflies and bumblebees live," she said. "I know what we can do!" Her tiara sparkled. She did a somersault. And suddenly a massive, peach-colored bumblebee was flying next to Clara. Flip the bumblebee looked at Clara

with giant, shiny eyes. "Now buzz as loudly as you can," she said in a high, vibrating voice.

Clara and Flip both made loud buzzing noises. Clara stopped when her nose started to itch from so much buzzing.

They waited and listened for a few seconds. Soon, loud buzzing echoed from the meadow below. "The bees are saying hi to us," Flip buzzed. "Want to see how bees dance?" She twittered her antennae and wiggled her stinger. Clara giggled and did a bee dance, too. Flip winked her enormous, shiny bee eye before she somersaulted to change back into a pegasus.

"Do you see that peach-colored cloud in the distance?" Flip asked, nodding ahead of them. "That's the entrance to the Magic Marsh."

Sure enough, if Clara squinted she could see a tiny peach dot in the sky ahead. She concentrated on flying as fast as she could toward the cloud, and she laughed as she bolted forward. "Wheeeeee!" she called out.

"Wow! You're fast," Flip said, zooming forward next to her. "And, speaking of fast, watch this." Flip's tiara sparkled. She did a somersault. And then a peach-colored chee-tah with dark peach spots raced through the sky next to Clara. Even her wings, Clara noticed with a grin, had spots. "Roar!" Flip called out.

"Roar!" Clara called out, pretending she was a lightning-quick cheetah.

Clara was surprised to hear roaring noises echoing in the distance.

"Those are the Wing Realm's wildcats,"

Flip meowed. "Don't worry. They're all very friendly."

Flip and Clara sped forward. The peach cloud in the distance grew larger and larger until it was right in front of them. Flip and Clara landed on the cloud, which felt slightly soggy, almost like thick mud, under Clara's sneakers. In the center of the cloud was a puddle of bubbling, peach-colored liquid. "I'd better go back to being a pegasus now," Flip said. "But thanks so much for pretending to be animals with me. It's one of my favorite games."

"I had fun too," Clara said. "Thank you."

Flip did a somersault and turned into a pegasus. For a few seconds, she whinnied, snorted, stomped her hooves, flicked her mane, swished her tail, and flapped her wings.

"What are you doing?" Clara asked.

Flip smiled self-consciously. "It always feels a little funny returning to my normal pegasus body after being so many different animals," she said. "I'm just getting used to being a pegasus again." She let out a final loud snort and stomped all four hooves as hard as she could. "Phew!" she said. "That's better now."

Flip looked at the gurgling puddle in front of them. "Getting into the Magic Marsh is always super fun," she said, with a grin. "Follow me!"

Flip bent her legs and leaped right into the middle of the puddle. In an enormous splash, Flip sank down into it and disappeared.

Chapter Five

Clara looked at the churning, gurgling puddle. She took a long, deep breath. She bent her knees. She closed her eyes. And then she jumped right into the center. For a split second, she sank deep into the puddle, so she felt as though she were in a swimming pool filled with warm, thick water. Just when she needed to take a breath, everything went pitch black and she felt as though she were falling through the air. Bright lights flashed. And then Clara was standing next to Flip on a wooden walkway. To her surprise, her clothes, skin, and hair were completely dry.

Clara blinked and put her hand on Flip's shoulder to steady herself. She felt a tiny bit dizzy.

"Welcome to the Magic Marsh," Flip said.

Clara sucked in her breath as she looked all around her. The wooden walkway cut across a field dotted with scarlet, crimson, magenta, and fuchsia puddles. The puddles gurgled and bubbled. They churned and swirled. They sprayed streams of liquid upward, reminding Clara of the fountains

in Feather Palace's front hall. Between the puddles grew clumps of star-shaped lavender flowers with long, stiff peacock-blue stems.

"The Magic Marsh is amazing," Clara whispered.

"I had a feeling you'd like it," Flip said.

A crimson puddle right next to Clara and Flip suddenly sprayed a stream of liquid straight upward. "Whoa," Clara said, stepping back and raising her eyebrows. "What kind of puddles are these?"

"They're wild potion puddles," Flip said as the puddle shot five jets of liquid into the air and then went back to bubbling. "There are some potions that creatures in the Wing Realm make and there are other

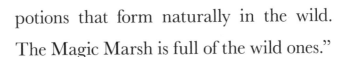

potions that form naturally in the wild. The Magic Marsh is full of the wild ones."

"Wow," Clara said. "And what are those star-shaped flowers?"

"They're wild wand flowers," Flip said. She smiled playfully. "Pick one and wave it in front of you."

Clara crouched at the edge of the walkway next to a cluster of wild wand flowers. She chose one with an especially long stem and an especially bright lavender star. She plucked it from the marsh, stood up, and waved the stem as though it were a magic wand. Instantly, the wand flower vanished. On the walkway, just in front of Clara's sneakers and Flip's hooves, appeared a pile of raspberries.

"The wild wand flowers all make different kinds of fruit," Flip said. "I have to admit, I was hoping for raspberries."

"Can we eat them?" Clara asked.

"Absolutely," Flip said.

Clara scooped up the raspberries. She put half of them in her mouth and held the other half out for Flip. She giggled at

the feeling of Flip's mouth gently eating the raspberries from her palms.

"Can we try one of the wild potion puddles, too?" Clara asked.

Flip shook her head. "I've learned the hard way that that's not a very good idea unless you know exactly what the potion does," Flip said, grimacing. "Once I sprinkled a wild potion on my head and ended up with stegosaurus spikes. And another time I ended up three weeks older. And another time I ended up wearing a very itchy ballet tutu that I couldn't get off. My sisters and I ended up spending a lot of time making an un-dinosaur potion, an un-time potion, and an un-ballet potion."

Clara giggled. "Is there any way to know

what the wild potions do without trying them?"

"Star can use her magic sense of hearing to figure it out. She listens to the gurgling sounds the puddles make and hears a message about what kind of potion it is," Flip said.

"That's amazing," Clara said. She took a few steps forward and kneeled on the edge of the walkway, right next to a magenta puddle that was making loud gurgling noises. She leaned right over it, closed her eyes, and tilted her head to the side so her ear was as close to the puddle as she could get it. She waited a few seconds. All she could hear was bubbling and gurgling.

"I think that one is about to spray potion

in the air," Flip said. "Back up before it sprays your head and we find out exactly what it does, whether we like it or not."

Clara opened her eyes, stood up, and took a step back. Sure enough, the puddle erupted into a fountain.

"I wish we could keep watching the puddles and playing with the wild wand flowers," Flip said. "But I think we'd better make sure everything is ready for the Potion Fair. We always hold the fair on top of that hill up ahead." Clara followed Flip's gaze to the far side of the marsh, where the walkway ended at a flight of white stone steps that led up the side of a grassy hill.

Clara nodded. "I'm ready to help in any

way I can," she said. "I can't wait to try all the potions at the Potion Fair."

"Me too," Flip said. "And I can't wait to show everyone else the flying potion my sisters and I invented. The creatures of the Wing Realm will love being able to fly without even flapping their wings."

Clara skipped and Flip trotted along the walkway across the marsh. They climbed together up the white stone steps to a wide, flat hilltop. At its center were large tree stumps arranged in a circle. "Each team puts its potion cauldron on one of the tree stumps," Flip explained. "Then we all walk around and sample each other's potions."

Clara nodded.

"The main thing we need to do is dust off the tree stumps," Flip said, galloping over to a stump and using her tail to sweep it off.

Clara skipped over to a different stump and used her hand to brush off dirt and moss. She moved on to the next stump, and as she whisked off a clump of moss, she heard the sound of wings beating the air. She turned and saw Star and Lucinda, both holding the peach cauldron's handle in their mouths, as they flew over the marsh toward the hill. Star and Lucinda landed next to a tree stump, where they carefully set down the cauldron.

"Phew!" Star said. "That cauldron is heavy."

"It sure is," Lucinda said, purring as she rubbed Clara's and Flip's ankles. "Sorry we're a little late. Star gave me six tries to guess her favorite part of outer space. I guessed asteroids, then planets, then moons, then black holes, then comets, and then meteoroids. I ran out of things to guess, so she told me the right answer. Can you believe the answer is stars? I was shocked." Lucinda widened her eyes in surprise and swished her tail.

Clara laughed and scratched Lucinda behind her ears. Lucinda turned and jumped onto the tree stump next to the cauldron. She stuck her head in it and sniffed. "I can smell the butterfly flutter in here," she said, purring and inhaling. "It

smells peppery to me. It always makes me—" Before she could finish her sentence, she sneezed five times in a row right into the potion.

"Well," she said, yawning as the potion in the cauldron began to bubble, "it's about time for my nap." She flew up into a tree behind the tree stump circle as the potion turned from green to blue. She flopped down onto a thick branch as the potion bubbled and frothed higher and higher. She closed her eyes as blue foam poured over the sides of the cauldron. She began to make a sound that was a cross between a purr and a snore as a flood of blue foam coated the hilltop and all the tree stumps. Lucinda was fast asleep when, in a swirl of

light, blue caterpillars appeared every-
where. They were all over the tree stumps.
They were all over the grass. There were
hundreds and hundreds and hundreds of
them.

Chapter Six

For several seconds, Flip, Star, and Clara stared at the sea of caterpillars. The caterpillars wiggled and crawled. They squirmed, rolled onto their backs, and kicked their legs. They twittered their antennae and grinned.

"Oh no," Flip said. "This is terrible."

"What a disaster," Star said. "I can't

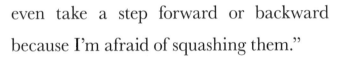

even take a step forward or backward because I'm afraid of squashing them."

Flip's eyes filled with tears. "We have no choice but to cancel the Potion Fair," she said in a high, wavering voice.

"All the creatures have worked so hard to invent their potions," Star said. "They'll feel so sad and disappointed."

"My favorite day of the year has turned into my least favorite day ever," Flip said, as tears streamed down her cheeks. "I'll go tell all the creatures who said they would be at the fair that it's canceled."

Star nodded. "I'll go back to Feather Palace and tell Mist, Aqua, Snow, Dash, Rosie, and Stitch not to bother coming."

"Wait," Clara said. "Before we cancel

the Potion Fair, let's just think for a few minutes about whether there is any way to quickly and safely move the caterpillars."

Flip nodded and let out a long sigh. "Good idea," she said. She furrowed her brow.

Star nodded and bit her lip.

Clara took a long deep breath. She looked down for a moment at the caterpillars as they wiggled, squirmed, twittered their antennae, grinned, and winked. They were, she had to admit, pretty cute. She glanced up at the spiral design on Flip's tiara and thought about the magic somersault Flip could do to turn into any animal. She looked at the star, moon, and planet design on Star's tiara and thought about her magical senses. She thought about the wild wand flowers and the wild potion puddles. And then, suddenly, Clara had an idea. She bent her knees to jump up and down with excitement, but then she stopped herself—she didn't want to accidentally crush the caterpillars when she landed. "I have an idea to save the Potion Fair," Clara said with wide, excited eyes. "I don't know if it will work. But we won't know unless we try."

"I'll do anything to help," Flip said, her eyes filling with hope.

"Me too," Star said. "Anything at all."

Clara smiled. She turned to Star. "Flip told me you can tell what the wild potion puddles do by listening to the gurgling noises they make."

"That's right," Star said, nodding.

"If we fly back to the marsh together, could you listen to the puddles and tell me what they do?" Clara asked.

"Sure," Star said. She flapped her wings and flew straight upward.

Clara imagined flying upward, and she instantly rose a few feet up into the air. She looked down and saw three caterpillars clinging to her left sneaker. Gently, she shook her shoe until the caterpillars fell to the ground.

Flip, Star, and Clara flew down to the marsh. Star hovered over a bubbling crimson puddle. Her tiara glittered. She closed her eyes and pricked up her ears as she listened to the bubbling noises. "This one is a shrinking potion," she announced.

Clara shook her head. "What's the next one?" she asked.

Star flew to a gurgling magenta one. Her tiara glittered. She closed her eyes, pricked up her ears, and listened. She smiled with amusement. "This one gives creatures unicorn horns."

Clara giggled. "That sounds like fun, but I don't think we need that one right now," she said. "What's the next one?"

Star flew to a fuchsia puddle. Her tiara glittered, she closed her eyes, and she listened for a few seconds. "This one makes time leap forward three weeks," she said.

"That's exactly what I was hoping for!" Clara said. She turned to Flip. "The next step is for you to turn yourself into a flying elephant," she said.

"An elephant?" Flip said, cocking her head to the side. "Are you sure?"

"I'm sure," Clara said with a wink.

Flip shrugged. The spiral design on her tiara sparkled. She flapped her wings, leaped into the air, and did a somersault. Suddenly, a giant peach elephant with wings hovered right next to Star and Clara.

Star giggled. "I don't think I've ever seen you turn into an elephant," she said.

Flip lifted her trunk and let out a loud, trumpeting noise.

"Do you think you could use your trunk like a straw to suck up that that potion puddle?" Clara asked.

"Sure," Flip trumpeted. She flew next to Star. She dipped the tip of her elephant trunk into the fuchsia puddle. Then, with a loud slurping noise, Flip sucked all of the puddle into her trunk.

"Excellent," Clara said. "Just don't swallow it by accident."

Clara swooped over to a cluster of wild wand flowers and picked one. "Now we're ready to go back to the caterpillars," she said.

Clara, Flip, and Star flew back to the hilltop. For a few seconds, they watched the squirming caterpillars. Clara turned to Flip. "Could you spray the potion in your trunk on all the caterpillars?" she asked.

Flip's eyes widened. She nodded. And then she flew in circles over the caterpillars, using her trunk to spray them with potion. Glittery pink light swirled around the caterpillars. And, in an instant, they were blue butterflies. The butterflies fluttered their wings. They hovered above the grass and tree stumps. They flew in small circles.

Clara took a long deep breath. "Perfect," she said.

"But now there are butterflies every-where," Star said, her face falling.

"I think they're looking for food," Flip trumpeted. "They probably feel like they haven't eaten in three weeks. But there are no real flowers here in the Magic Marsh. Just the wild wand flowers. And they don't have nectar." Tears welled up again in her eyes. "I still think we'll have to cancel the Potion Fair."

"We're not quite done with my plan yet," Clara said. "I have to admit that I'm not as sure the next part will work. But let's give it a try." She turned to Flip and raised her eyebrows. "Can you turn into a giant mother kangaroo now?"

Flip's giant forehead wrinkled in confusion. She shrugged her shoulders and let out one last elephant trumpet before she did a somersault and turned back into a pegasus. Then, the spiral design on her tiara glittered. She did another somersault. Suddenly a large peach kangaroo with wings and a pouch hovered next to Clara.

"Perfect!" Clara said. "Now, could you please hold your pouch as far open as possible?"

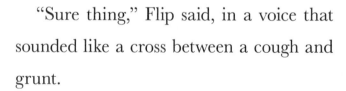

"Sure thing," Flip said, in a voice that sounded like a cross between a cough and grunt.

Clara giggled—she had always wondered what sound kangaroos made!

Flip used her front paw to pull her pouch open. Clara held up the wild wand flower she had picked in the marsh and waved it right above the pouch. A giant slice of watermelon appeared in the bottom of Flip's pouch. For a few seconds, nothing happened. Clara held her breath and stared at the swarming butterflies. But then, to her relief, the hungry butterflies smelled the watermelon. They waved their antennae in excitement. They swarmed and fluttered in circles around Flip's giant kangaroo body. And then, all at once, they dived into her pouch, carefully closing their wings, to eat the watermelon.

Flip and Star exchanged looks of amazement.

"Remember that meadow of wild-flowers we flew over on the way here?" Clara asked Flip.

Flip nodded. "The one where we buzzed to the bees?" she grunted.

"Exactly," Clara said. "Do you think you could fly there, holding your pouch open so you don't crush the butterflies, and release them?"

"That's an amazing idea," Flip grunted.

"I'll be right back." With one paw holding her pouch open, she zoomed away from the hill. Clara and Star flew down to the ground as they watched Flip disappear over the Magic Marsh.

"Thank you so much for saving the Potion Fair," Star said to Clara. "That was one of the strangest, funniest plans that I can imagine. Who knew we'd need an elephant and a kangaroo to save the Potion Fair from caterpillars?"

"It was my pleasure to help," Clara said. She peered into the pegasus princesses' now-empty cauldron. Every drop of the potion had turned into caterpillars. She looked over at Star, who had busied herself dusting off a stump with her tail. "Remember how we divided the potion in half this morning? Why don't you go get the other half so you'll still have some potion to share with the other creatures?" Clara smiled reassuringly and shrugged. "It's okay with me if there isn't any left for my next visit. Besides, we can always make more if we need to."

"Good idea," Star said. "Thank you, Clara. I'll take this cauldron back to Feather Palace and bring back the other one. If I fly my very fastest, I'll be back in no time. I'll get my sisters to join me."

"Sounds great," Clara said. "I'll finish sweeping off the tree stumps."

Star flapped her wings, and, in a blur of black, flew back toward Feather Palace.

Chapter Seven

C lara had just finished sweeping off the last tree stump when she heard the sound of wings. She turned to see seven pegasus princesses and one giant peach kangaroo flying toward her. Star and Aqua, holding a shiny peach cauldron together in their mouths, flew straight to a tree stump and set down the cauldron. Flip, Mist, Rosie, Stitch, Dash, and

Snow gathered in a circle around the tree stump. "The butterflies are safely in the flower garden," Flip grunted. "Thank you so much for saving the Potion Fair. What a wacky, creative idea you had. But it worked!"

"Star told us the whole story," Mist said.

"Thank you so much for everything you've done to help us," Snow said.

Dash, Stitch, Rosie, and Aqua nodded and swished their tails.

"I'm so glad I could help," Clara said.

Star looked at Flip. "Um," she said, "it's perfectly fine if you want to be a kangaroo for the Potion Fair. But I think you could probably turn back into a pegasus now if you wanted to."

"Huh?" Flip grunted. Then she looked

down at her kangaroo paws, her pouch, her long tail, and her enormous hind legs. She laughed. "Oops! I completely forgot to turn back into a pegasus," she grunted. "Just a second!" She did a giant kangaroo bounce into the air. She somersaulted. In an instant, she was a pegasus again. Flip stomped her hooves, whinnied, snorted, and flicked her mane. "I'm glad to be my normal self," she said with a smile.

"Did I miss anything?" a voice purred. Clara turned to see Lucinda standing up on her tree branch. She arched her back and stretched forward.

Clara and the pegasus princesses looked at each other. Clara raised her eyebrows. The pegasus princesses smiled.

"Not too much," Flip said.

Lucinda leaped out of the tree and sauntered over to Clara and the pegasus princesses. She leaped onto the tree stump and peered into the cauldron. She sniffed several times and then Clara heard her making an "*AH! AH! AH!*" sound. Lucinda was about to sneeze! Clara spun around and quickly lifted the cauldron up over her head just as Lucinda sneezed five times in a row.

All eight pegasus princesses stared as Lucinda sat down on the tree stump and began licking her front foot. They looked at Clara, who still held the cauldron safely up above her head. After a few seconds of shocked silence, Clara, Flip, Star, Mist,

Aqua, Rosie, Dash, Stitch, and Snow burst out laughing.

"Now you've saved the Potion Fair twice!" Flip said.

"And just in the nick of time," Star said, nodding toward a parade of creatures flying into the meadow carrying cauldrons. There were teams of merfairies, phoenixes, winged frogs, fairies, dragons, winged foxes, and winged squirrels. Each group flew to a tree stump and put down its cauldron.

"Lucinda," Clara said, "might I put the cauldron back down on the tree stump now?"

"Absolutely," Lucinda purred, moving to one side.

"Um—" Flip began.

"It's just that—" Star said.

"Well—" Mist said.

"We really want you to be part of the Potion Fair," Clara said. "But do you think you could stay away from the cauldron? Just so you don't sneeze in it."

Lucinda swished her tail. "Well," she purred. "I suppose I could do that." She leaped off the tree stump, and Clara put down the potion.

Flip looked at Clara. "Now we get to walk around and try all the different potions. Want to come with me?"

Clara hopped up and down with excitement. "Yes," she said. "I can't wait."

"We can take turns standing next to our cauldron," Mist said. "I'm happy to stay

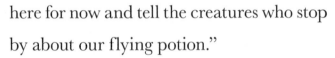

here for now and tell the creatures who stop by about our flying potion."

"Thank you," Flip said. She looked at Clara. "Let's go test out the frogs' potion."

"Okay," Clara said. She and Flip walked to the tree stump next to theirs, where three purple frogs with gold wings sat next to a green cauldron.

"Want to try our potion?" one of the frogs croaked.

"It will turn you purple for five seconds," another frog croaked.

Clara and Flip nodded and laughed. Clara dipped her hand into the cauldron, where a violet liquid bubbled. She sprinkled the potion on her head and on Flip's head. After a split second, both Clara and

Flip were purple. Clara looked at her purple hands and fingernails. She grabbed a strand of her hair, and was delighted to see that even it looked purple. And then, all of a sudden, the purple was gone.

"That was fun," Flip said to the frogs. "Thanks so much."

"Our pleasure," the frogs croaked back.

"Now let's try the foxes' potion," Flip suggested.

"Sounds great," Clara said, skipping alongside Flip over to the foxes' tree stump.

A bright orange fox standing next to a yellow cauldron grinned invitingly. "The potion we invented will make you able to stand upside down for ten seconds," explained the fox.

"I've never done that before," Flip said.

"Me either," Clara said. "Let's try it." She dipped her hand into the cauldron and sprinkled orange potion on Flip's head and on her head. Clara looked at Flip and raised her eyebrows. "Here I go!" she sang out. She put her hands on the grassy ground. She pulled her legs upward as though she were about to do a cartwheel— but then she found she could easily keep her legs up in the air. She was doing a handstand! Clara took several steps forward on her hands, giggling with delight. She looked over to see that Flip was walking on her front hooves with her back hooves up in the air. "This is amazing," Flip said, doing a dance on her front hooves.

"It's so much fun," Clara said.

The potion wore off, and Clara's legs gently returned to the ground. Flip stood next to her on all four hooves.

Flip and Clara walked the rest of the way around the fair. They tried a dragon potion that let them breathe lukewarm blue fire for twenty seconds. They tried a mer-fairy potion that gave them amazing singing voices for three minutes. They tried a phoenix potion that made their hands and hooves into talons for fifteen seconds. They tried a fairy potion that made them shrink to the size of acorns for thirty seconds. And they tried a squirrel potion that gave them giant, bushy tails for a minute.

Clara loved trying all the potions, but

she was beginning to miss Miranda. Plus, she felt ready to help her sister finish making their potion by the creek.

"I hate to say this," Clara said to Flip, "but I'm ready to go home to the Human World."

"I completely understand," Flip said. "Thank you so much for joining us and for saving the Potion Fair!"

"Yes, thank you for coming," Star said, galloping over.

Stitch and Snow, both purple, trotted over to Clara. "Come again soon," they said at the same time, just as the purple wore off and they went back to being green and white.

Dash walked upside down on her front

legs over to Clara. "We've loved having you join us today," she said.

"It really was wonderful to see you again," Aqua and Rosie said as blue flames came out of their mouths and nostrils.

Clara looked down as Lucinda, who was the size of an acorn, wove between Clara's ankles. "Goodbye, Clara," Lucinda purred. "Do you promise to play another guessing game with me again soon?"

"Absolutely," Clara said, giving the cat a final scratch behind her silver ears.

Clara pulled the magic silver feather from the pocket of her peach skirt. "I want to fly one last time," she said, smiling. She imagined flying up into the air, and she giggled as her body lifted upward. Hovering right above the pegasus princesses, she did a somersault and flew in a final circle. Then, she carefully gripped the feather in both hands and said, "Take me home please."

The feather lifted Clara up into the air. She felt herself spinning, faster and faster. Everything went pitch black. And then she was sitting under a pine tree in the forest surrounding her house. Clara smiled. She stood up. Something heavy was in her skirt pocket. She pushed her hand in and pulled out two purple mixing spoons, just like the ones in Feather Laboratory. Clara grinned. She couldn't wait to share them with her sister. She leaped with joy. And then she jogged back toward the creek where Miranda was waiting.

Don't miss our next high-flying adventure!

Turn the page for a sneak peek . . .

Clara sucked in her breath as she admired the front hall of Feather Palace. Painted portraits of the eight pegasus princesses and their pet cat, Lucinda, hung on the magenta walls. Chandeliers cast sparkling light on the black tile floors. Pegasus fountains spouted rainbow water. Pegasus sculptures reared up, wings outstretched, from pedestals. In the center of the room, arranged in a half-circle, were the pegasus princesses' eight thrones. Lucinda's sofa—silver with a back shaped like a cat head—was pushed up against Star's throne. And on it Lucinda lay curled in a tight ball, fast asleep.

Clara looked around the front hall for the pegasus princesses. And then she spotted them next to an open window, huddled around what looked like a purple telescope with eight eyepieces. For a few

seconds, Clara watched her friends. And then she called out, "Hello!"

The pegasus princesses jumped in surprise and turned around. As soon as they saw Clara, they reared up, whinnied, and galloped over to her.

"I'm thrilled you're here," Star said, hopping from side to side. "You've arrived just in time."

"Welcome back, human friend," Mist said, trotting in a circle around Clara.

"We've been hoping you would come," Aqua said.

"We have a fun afternoon planned," Dash whispered.

Rosie nodded.

Flip winked.

Stitch and Snow swished their tails.

"I can't wait to tell you what we're doing this afternoon," Star said in a soft voice. "But I'm going to have to whisper it into your ear so *someone*—" Star paused and glanced over at Lucinda, who was still asleep, "doesn't hear. Every once in a while, she pretends to be asleep."

The other seven pegasus princesses grinned and nodded.

Star leaned up to Clara's ear and whispered, "Today is Lucinda's birthday, and I have organized a surprise party for her. Would you like to join us?"

"Yes!" Clara whispered in a voice that

was a little too loud. Clara blushed. She had never been good at whispering.

Star laughed. "I had a feeling you'd say yes," she said. "Are you ready for the best part?"

Clara's eyes widened. She nodded.

"We are holding the party with Lucinda's six cousins, the mooncats, on the Catmoon," Star whispered.

Clara raised her eyebrows. "What is the Catmoon?" she asked.

"It's the Wing Realm's very own moon. We were just looking at it through the octogoloctoscope," Star said, now using her normal voice. "Would you like to see it?"

"Definitely," Clara said.

"Come right this way," Star said, and

she trotted over to the instrument Clara had thought looked like a telescope. "We used to have a normal monogoloctoscope with just one eyepiece," Star explained. "But my sisters and I spent so much time arguing over whose turn it was to use it that we decided to get this one. Pick any eyepiece and look through it."

Clara leaned toward one of the octogoloctoscope's eyepieces. She closed her left eye and looked through it with her right eye. Clara sucked in her breath with delight. Hanging against a dark lavender backdrop was a silver ball with two mountains that looked like cat ears and two giant green lakes that looked like cat eyes.

"Do you see it?" Star asked.

"Yes," Clara said. "I had no idea the Wing Realm even had a moon."

Star leaned toward Clara's ear and whispered, "We told Lucinda we're all traveling to the Catmoon this afternoon to help her cousins clean their castle. She's irritated she has to do chores on her birthday. She'll be surprised when she discovers we're throwing a party for her instead."

"Clara?" a sleepy voice purred. "Is that you?"

Emily Bliss, also the author of the Unicorn Princesses series, lives with her winged cat in a house surrounded by woods. From her living room window, she can see silver feathers and green flying armchairs. Like Clara Griffin, she knows pegasuses are real.

Sydney Hanson was raised in Minnesota alongside numerous pets and brothers. She is the illustrator of the Unicorn Princesses series and the picture books *Next to You, Escargot,* and *A Book for Escargot,* among many others. Sydney lives in Los Angeles.

www.sydwiki.tumblr.com

HENRY JAMES

The Creative Process

HENRY JAMES
(*Drawing by Julio Granda*)

HENRY JAMES

JAMES

The Creative Process

by

HAROLD T. McCARTHY

New York • THOMAS YOSELOFF • London

To
DONALD S. TAYLOR

Foreword

WHILE HENRY JAMES HAD LITTLE INTEREST IN FORMAL AESTHETICS
per se, he was a dedicated artist and student of art from the
earliest stage of his career. He was concerned not only with exploring the technical possibilities of his craft, but also with
understanding the nature and function of the creative process
itself. Consequently, his writings evince a preoccupation with
such matters as the relation of art to experience, the importance
of aesthetic perceptions for art, the operation of feeling in the
creative process and in the work of art. Other questions of an
aesthetic nature, specifically related to the process of expression, concerned James. They dealt with the dramatic development of the substance of a work and the organic nature of its
form. These matters are dealt with in the first six chapters of
this study. Chapter Seven attempts to illustrate the relation of
James's "method" to his aesthetic theories by a discussion of his
highly characteristic use of a ghostly element, ambiguity, and a
sense of the past. Chapter Eight is concerned with James's concept of prose as an aesthetic medium. The last two chapters deal
with aesthetic considerations underlying James's deep concern
with the relation of the artist to his work and to society.

7

I have based this study upon all of James's available writing: fiction, reviews, critical articles, biographies, letters, notebooks, autobiographical books, and other works extending through a period of over fifty years. It attempts to indicate the evolution of his ideas, but one must bear in mind that James had no systematic and abstract set of theories; that some ideas changed little throughout his career, while others changed greatly. A synthesis has been necessary because James rarely dealt at length with the theory of art; his views usually emerge indirectly in his discussion of the work of other writers, or in an exegesis of his own creative problems, or in a dramatized form. The body of opinions he held from the time he was, say, forty on strengthened and broadened, however, and modified only in details.

This study deals with all the major aspects of James's aesthetics. The selection of material has been determined by his interest in aesthetic matters as this was manifested in his writing throughout his career. All references are to James's works, and the terminology is that employed by James himself in what is, viewed as a whole, perhaps the most lucid and thorough analysis in any language by an artist of his art.

Contents

HENRY JAMES

The Creative Process

*This profuse development of the external percep-
tions—those of the appearance, the sound, the
taste, the material presence and pressure of things,
will at any rate, I think, not be denied to be the
master-sign of the novel in France as the first
among the younger talents show it to us to-day.
They carry into the whole business of looking, seeing, hearing, smelling, into all kinds of tactile sensibility and into noting, analyzing, and expressing
the results of these acts, a seriousness much greater
than that of any other people. Their tactile sensibility is immense, and it may be said in truth to
have produced a literature. They are so strong on
this side that they seem to me to be easily masters,
and I cannot imagine that their supremacy should
candidly be contested. James,* Essays in London,
"Pierre Loti."*

The Sensuous Surface

THE NEED OF THE ARTIST "TO LIVE . . . TO HAVE HIS EXPERIENCE,"
forms one of the central themes in Henry James's fiction, and
it is a belief to which he persistently returns in his extensive
discussions of art. James believed that the artist should cultivate his sense impressions and then carefully analyze them, go
beneath appearances to discover what they might disclose about
life in general. Thus, the *use* to which an artist put his experience was of the utmost importance, but first of all came the
need to have sharply realized impressions. The three autobiographical books which James wrote during his last years parade
a colorful series of impressions registered in his childhood and
adolescence. These books testify as well as anything might to
James's extraordinary capacity for retaining his impressions of
life and for exploring their significance. Despite the crowded
half-century that intervened, when the time came to use them

he found them still aesthetically vivid enough to permit him "the act of life."

So keen was his recollection of these early years that his reminiscence is a mixed blessing to the student of James's life. James selected and arranged his material so as to emphasize certain conditions and obscure others. One condition, however, which James insists on frequently, and which there seems to be no reason to doubt, is his astonishing sensitivity to impressions and his habit of storing them in his mind until they had given up their deepest meaning.

The kind of education which Henry James received as a child was one beautifully adapted to supplying him with sensuous impressions that were worth preserving. There was comparatively little formal education in the lives of the James children; and where Henry was concerned this was just as well, for he appeared to respond hardly at all to instruction that appealed to his intellect alone. He apparently gained little from successive schools and tutors, while he benefited enormously from his own discursive reading and from the long visits which the James family paid to Europe. During the years 1855–58 and 1859–60, when most of the boys of his age and social standing were preparing for college under a carefully regulated discipline, James was moving about Europe, enjoying a succession of tutors, schools, and responding to the cultural patterns of England, France, Switzerland, Germany, and Italy. In a way it is not at all strange that James should be found in the year 1862 enrolled as a student at the Harvard Law School. The instruction dispensed there was no more alien to him than many another he had previously been exposed to, and, as always, he used the occasion as an opportunity to study character, to register "appearances."

The student body at Harvard Law School splendidly suited

this purpose, and James found himself so besieged by impressions of the sort he was seeking that instead of having to search painstakingly for them: ". . . I had much rather to steady myself, at any moment, where I stood." It was at this time that James first encountered James Russell Lowell. Instead of burrowing into law books, James preferred to spend his winter afternoons attending Lowell's lectures on English literature and Old French, and he was never to forget the charm of these occasions. It would appear, too, that Balzac claimed a great deal of James's attention at this time. He had the habit of equating the people and places he encountered in real life with the characters and scenes that lived for him in fiction. The extremes his youthful imagination could reach in these equations is suggested by the fact that the genteel boarding-house he frequented during this period, one attended by several other well-bred students, took on for him the aspect of the squalid Maison Vauquer in Balzac's *Le Père Goriot.*

All the while he was at Harvard Law School and for several years earlier, James had been trying to write stories and plays. He even sent some of his efforts to publishers, but it was not until 1865, with the publication of *The Story of a Year* in *The Atlantic Monthly,* that he publicly proclaimed himself an author and launched his career as a writer of fiction. James's early stories are brilliant in comparison with the stories then being published in America, but despite his sensitivity to impressions and his capacity for analyzing them, he failed to make satisfactory use of his experience in the stories he published up through 1869.

This failure was due largely to his inability to find a satisfactory method of coping with the American scene. There was no available tradition that could supply him with instruction and inspiration on the problem of expressing his experience in artistic form. American material treated in terms of the characters and settings to be found in European fiction seemed both false and foolish. James's first published review commenced with an expression of regret that there was no critical treatise on fiction.

On the other hand, it seemed to James that material for fiction abounded in America. In later years he remembered the period as one in which more appearances, "felt aspects, images, apprehended living relations and impressions of the stress of life" were at his command than at any other period of his life. But he did not yet have the ability to express this material, and his attempts were not very successful. He wanted to deal with subtleties of motivation and with delicate moral impulses; he wanted to suggest through a few details a great deal about the kind of people his characters were and the true significance of their actions. He found himself severely handicapped, however, because he could not resort to the convenient apparatus of manners and traditions constantly employed by the European novelists he so much admired. When he tried to finesse his problem by employing the manner of George Sand, the results were embarrassingly unsuccessful. Even his attempt to use the devices of Hawthorne, as in *A Romance of Certain Old Clothes*, resulted in a rather trivial "ghost-story," utterly lacking in the metaphysical depth of his models.

The Story of a Year and *A Romance of Certain Old Clothes*, like the other short stories he was to write during this early period, had American settings. So did his first novel, *Watch and Ward* (1871). James did not feel that the effect was satisfactory. It seemed to him that he would be far better off if he situated his stories in Europe. He could trust his American impressions more confidently for other components of his stories. Between the years 1870 and 1875, after which James went to reside permanently in Europe, he spent a great deal of time in Italy, as well as long periods in France and England. During this time, he published fourteen stories, six of which are connected with Italy and four with other European countries. James was well aware that in situating his stories in Europe, in using the European setting in preference to the American, he was taking the easy way out.

James found the American scene crammed with material for fiction; the difficulty lay in capturing the tone of American life. The varieties and intensities were there, but they were obscured by an apparent uniformity and an abounding confusion, so that a most unusual ability was required to deal with them. America was "a very sufficient literary field," but "it will yield its secrets only to a really *grasping* imagination," he noted.

In Europe the forces that had gone into the shaping of civilization were manifest to James's senses at every turn. Everything from castles and cathedrals to turns of speech and eccentricities of dress bespoke numberless relations that could be put to use in art. The mere mention of the names Paris, London, Rome was like a magician's phrase that did half the artist's work of persuading the reader to accept illusion for reality. By contrast, the artist who would be successful with American material was thrown completely upon his own resources. "To write well and worthily of American things," James observed in 1871, "one needs more than elsewhere to be a *master*." And masters did not abound. Again and again in his early reviews James was tempted to rearrange the stories, to alter plots, tamper with endings, stress different characters and situations. The prose fiction he reviewed dealt so sketchily with American life that he was often exasperated by its blindness.

Despite James's comments on the multiplicity of his impressions of American life, he was ignorant of many important phases of it. His willingness to accept for contemplation whatever chanced to offer itself, instead of actively investigating the life about him, contributed to this limitation. Another important factor, too, was the number of years he had spent in Europe, an experience that set up powerful counter-attractions to life in Cambridge, Newport, and New York. To some extent these factors account for James's indifference to one important strand of what novel tradition did exist in America. C. B. Brown, Cooper, and Hawthorne had all felt a conscious obligation to make the substance of their work essentially American and especially to reproduce typical scenes of American life. It is probable that at this stage James would have considered such a tradition provincial and one which limited the moral possibilities of art.

It was James's good fortune that the segment of American life which he knew most thoroughly was the one most vital to America's spiritual and cultural life. Consequently, even if he did not make use of American settings, he could still make a searching criticism of American life when dealing with America only by implication and through the contrast afforded by a European milieu. By the end of the seventies he was enough a master of his craft to employ American settings with success, as in *The Europeans* (1878) and *Washington Square* (1880), but by this time many other considerations were at work to dictate his use of the European scene.

Aside from the matter of settings, there were other important aspects of American prose that concerned James during this early period. He exhibited, for example, a concern with the aesthetic quality of prose, a subject that had received scarcely any attention in American letters prior to Emerson. James not only noted Emerson's observations on language, but gave careful scrutiny to the concrete images and sustained aesthetic appeal to be found in his writing. The haphazard use of description and the careless use of words were matters that James sharply attacked in his reviews of contemporary fiction. He carefully studied Hawthorne's use of symbols. In these and other ways he manifested his concern with the sensuous surface he wished to achieve in his own writing, a concern that was soon to be intensified by his acquaintance with the new school of realism in France. Prior to this initiation, however, James's desire to see ideas take some plastic form, to find expression in prose images that appealed to the senses, was something he acquired in large measure from a close reading of New England writers such as Emerson and Thoreau, who practiced the transcendentalist theory that the idea and the concrete word should be one.

James also admired Hawthorne's ability to treat material that was part and parcel of the daily life of his readers. Hawthorne had the kind of grasping imagination that could seize the meanings that lay behind the confused sameness of American life; he could look upon the familiar life of a simple New England town and see flickering through the quiet surface which it presented to the world the ancient fires and shadows of evil. "He saw the quaintness or the weirdness, the interest *behind* the interest," and saw it immanent in everyday life, not as something abstract or remote.

It can be said, then, that James found a good deal to admire in American writing where aesthetic qualities were concerned. Of the writers of the day, he singled out William Dean Howells for especial praise as one who, if he did not probe deeply, at least secured an effective sensuous surface in his fiction. This was far more than could be said for the English novelists, James felt. The English novelists probed deeply enough, but their writing remained vague and abstract for the most part. James wanted to hear, to feel, above all to see, and all too often English writers muffled his senses in the impalpable constructions of philosophy. They ordered this matter differently in France.

When James went to live in Europe permanently, he began a crucial phase in his life as an artist. He was no longer an isolated spirit involved in mystic, solitary rites. The novel was clearly recognized by the leading literary men in France as a distinct art form with its own peculiar problems and possibilities. The new school of realism was well under way with Flaubert as its recognized master and with *Madame Bovary* as its cornerstone. James had watched the progress of their work from afar, alternately excited by their brilliance and dismayed by their immorality. Now he was on the scene, and if he held himself apart from individual literary groups, he nevertheless felt that he shared their dedication to the literary craft. Here was to be found the company of highly cultivated men whose most serious concern was the reading and writing of prose-fiction.

By the winter of 1875–76 James had advanced so far in the literary world as to be taken by no less a personage than Turgenieff to meetings of the Flaubert *cénacle,* but he was far from yielding himself up as a devotee of the group. Most of the great names associated with the French novel in the last quarter of the century gathered for the discussions held on Sunday afternoons at Flaubert's apartment in Paris. Zola, Edmond de Goncourt, Alphonse Daudet were there, and to many a young writer the effect would have been overpowering. The young Guy de Maupassant, who had yet to make his mark, was there and his relationship with Flaubert was practically that of father and son.

James admired the discussions of technique that took place, particularly since they dwelt so much on the question of how to produce successful sensuous effects. The French novelists seemed unaware, however, of many other matters relevant to art, matters that seemed vital to him. That their discussion should be limited to the French novel alone was to him an inexcusable provincialism. It was a judicious appraisal of such meetings and not vanity that led James to write to his father about the leader of the group, Flaubert, "I think I easily—more than easily—see all round him intellectually."

There were decided limitations, James recognized, to what the French realists could offer him, but even so the offering was of great value. He could observe the actual process of gifted writers converting their experience into art. He could hear, at first hand, their analysis of one another's work. He could study closely their method of turning impressions into a brilliant pattern of prose images, of bringing to the reader's eyes, ears, even to his nose, an awareness of the people and places they wrote about. It would have been perverse not to respond to such a sustained and powerful aesthetic appeal. As no novelists before them, they were concerned with the exact word, the precise image, the significant detail; whether sordid or gay, life glittered in their pages. The one great novelist of the past who was worshiped by this group was Balzac, and Balzac had long been one of James's idols. Like Melville in America, Stendhal had almost completely disappeared from the literary scene. Balzac, Flaubert, and the latter's immediate followers dominated the stage. James's successive critical examinations of these authors reveals the evolution of his opinion on the relation of art to experience and, more particularly, on the aesthetic expression of experience.

During James's early years as a reviewer, he had expressed his opinion that Balzac was a genuine observer, a writer whose observations were rooted in historical truth. By the time he had come to live in Europe, however, James's personal sense of things led him to believe that much of Balzac's historical truth was only clever fakery. James's knowledge of the French aristocracy was, by his own testimony in the "Preface" to *The American,* somewhat shaky at this stage, but it was sufficiently sound for him to determine that much of the experience which Balzac so glibly incorporated into his work was completely invented, especially where that experience concerned "high-life," the life of the salons, of the old aristocracy. To handle this life demanded first-hand observation plus a high degree of taste and a sense for charm—qualities which James felt Balzac did not possess.

James was much later to rescind, in part, this view of Balzac. He decided finally that Balzac must have relied heavily upon personal experience, and that the vast accumulation of life in his pages could only be accounted for by accrediting him with a sense for facts, an inspiration and intuition that absorbed the scene about him in a way comparable to nothing ever shown before. Hardly anything that touched him was wasted; all went into his art. But the failure in regard to taste and the insensitivity to charm remained, in James's judgment, and were transmitted to Balzac's followers.

The lesson which James learned from the study of Balzac's shortcomings was the necessity of never simply taking experience as it comes, or taking it for granted. This was particularly true when experience bore upon the inward life of the mind, the *"cultivated* consciousness." The fragments of experience vouchsafed the writer in this connection need to be patiently analyzed, compared, until whatever shy, furtive hints they may contain are felt and understood. Only on the basis of this careful and protracted examination is the artist free to construct his hypotheses concerning human conditions that are subtle, complex, and rarely to be observed. There is no room for stereotyped treatment here. The intelligence is given the widest possible play in order to convert the hints supplied by experience into revelations. The artist's treatment of his experience becomes a process of discovery, rewarding him with freshly conceived possibilities, a vision of ideals hitherto unimagined.

Since Flaubert was not only the chief literary descendant of Balzac, but *cher maître* of the new school, James gave him careful attention. It is revealing to observe James's speculations on Flaubert's efforts to convert his experience into literature, and his concern with the aesthetic quality of his prose. Like Balzac, James noted, Flaubert had been concerned almost exclusively with the "outside" of things, accepting only what was presented to the eyes, while the Goncourts reduced this technique to an absurdity. The writings of the latter were merely clever concoctions, a product almost exclusively of the studio; even their "realism" was artificial. In his 1876 study of Flaubert, James set forth what he considered to be Flaubert's theory of writing. He stressed the importance which Flaubert placed upon reporting things, all things, as they appeared to the eye. He stressed, too, Flaubert's failure to emphasize the selection and analysis of observations, his willingness to accept appearances as incapable of improvement, his belief that the observation was an ultimate fact that must appear as such in the novel. James rejoiced that *Madame Bovary* appeared before Flaubert had formed his theory.

When James again touched upon Flaubert, in the course of an essay on Turgenieff he wrote in 1884, his tone was one of sincere compassion for Flaubert. He now felt that it was some psychological difficulty that interfered with Flaubert's creative process and prevented him from examining certain areas of experience. In 1893 James developed this point of view further, claiming that both in his life and in his writings Flaubert "failed of happiness, failed of temperance, not through his excesses but through his barriers." He quoted from one of Flaubert's letters to the effect that he was in his youth *"afraid* of life," in partial support of a conclusion that Flaubert did not trust himself to treat the tender, nobler aspects of experience. James decided that Flaubert dealt with the remote and strange because it was his only alternative to dealing with the immediate and ugly. Even the process of writing was a labor unattended with any happiness for Flaubert, and this saddened James, who looked upon writing as a labor of love and rejoiced in its very difficulties.

For James the act of writing was an act of life which brought, amongst other rewards, that of personal happiness. This was not simply something in the nature of a reward that came after a successful stretch of exposition; it was a condition that attached to the writing experience itself. It seemed that through expressing his feelings and ideas aesthetically, working them into an art-form both as true and as beautiful as possible, he strengthened his mental faculties and his spiritual awareness. Writing became an experience of growth and purification. The gloomy aspects of French life which Flaubert chose to discuss, and the high artistic standards he set for himself were not things unfamiliar to James. He, too, repeatedly drew his *donnée* from a context of evil, and the artistic standards he set for himself were deliberately made to bristle with difficulties. But James never remained passive before evil; as an artist he set to work to construct aesthetically its counterpart in the good.

To include only what was noble in human experience would have seemed to James as pointless as to include only what was base. Both were present in human experience, and the artist who pretended to deal honestly with life had no right to exclude the one or the other. When such a magnificent stylist as Flaubert consecrated his art to working over the commonplace and gross aspects of human nature, he perpetuated an aesthetic experience that was seriously incomplete. At least, James felt, Flaubert should have listened "at the chamber of the soul."

The views which James manifests in discussing the relation between Flaubert's experience and his art apply with slight alterations to Guy de Maupassant. As the most devoted of Flaubert's followers, Maupassant attended the master's Sunday gatherings for years before *Boule de Suif* brought him overnight a reputation as a gifted writer. It was there James met him and possibly heard some of the tales with which Maupassant delighted Flaubert and other members of the group, tales of his lively sexual adventures with the girls who frequented the boating-clubs along the Seine. Possibly these early encounters with Maupassant influenced James's opinion of the man as a writer, for James was to insist that Maupassant's knowledge of human motives was limited to the sexual impulse.

Almost in the same breath with which he deplored Flaubert's and Maupassant's limited experience and the unfortunate direction their taste seemed compelled to take, James called attention to the perfection achieved by certain of their works. Their stylistic achievements alone, James asserted, would serve to sustain interest in their work. Of all their literary gifts, the one he singled out as most important was "a remarkable art of expressing the life, of picturing the multitudinous, adventurous experience of the senses." Writers of Flaubert's school failed to go behind appearances to the "deeper, stranger, subtler inward life," but they displayed an acute aesthetic awareness and the ability to present effectively the testimony of their senses. This aesthetic achievement was described by James as "the master-sign of the novel in France as the first among the younger talents show it to us today."

Strictly speaking there was no such thing as a "Flaubert

school," and Flaubert would have been the last to promote such a thing—especially in the way, for example, that Zola set about organizing the cult of "Naturalism." Practically all of the writers who associated with Flaubert, however, sought to achieve the kind of sensuous surface in their work that impressed James so deeply. Yet, the very brilliance and precision of their details could be a flaw, to James's mind, if the details had reference to nothing more than themselves. Balzac spoke, in *Père Goriot,* of "the diorama, an exhibition which carried optical illusion beyond that of the panorama." James seized on the term to describe the way in which a sensory detail served when properly used in a novel. It had its immediate sensory reference, but it also brought into focus other references of a more general nature to illuminate and enrich the whole work. The description of a dress supplied a clue to the character of the wearer; the description of a room might characterize the inhabitant; the description of a garden or the countryside might contribute to the reader's understanding of a moral situation or emotional crisis, and so forth. All too frequently James found that details in the work of the French novelists served no such "dioramic" function; the detail of color, smell, sound or taste only served to call attention to itself.

Pierre Loti's work brought the reader into the fishing ports of Brittany; Maupassant brought him magically to Normandy. Such localization was well and good, but it could easily be overdone. When this happened, full appreciation of the work was apt to be restricted to those who knew the locale. Alphonse Daudet's work, it seemed to James, had its full value only for people who were intimate with the Parisian scene. The lesson to be learned from this was that the part had to be subordinated to the whole. A vivid detail, an admirably depicted scene was of greater value when it contributed to the general theme of the work of art.

If James felt that for his own purposes the sensuous surface should be made to illustrate something of more significance than itself alone, he nevertheless was quick to grant that in cases such as Daudet's, the brilliance of the aesthetic texture alone was sufficient to cause his work to endure. The great French novelists of the period, however restricted their experience might be, were artists. This was a claim that the English novelists could not make, even though they dealt so much with the moral and spiritual nature of man. The advantage belonged to the French, and they would keep their advantage, James opined, ". . . till the optimists of the hour, the writers for whom the life of the soul is equally real and visible (lends itself to effects and triumphs, challenges the power to 'render'), begin to seem to them formidable competitors."

James remained an "optimist" in full awareness of the sordid social conditions that provided the material of so many French novels. He saw this material as material for change. He believed in the possibility of social reform, and he was convinced that the artist was not limited to reproducing what he saw, that he could transmute his material. James saw the decay, but he also saw the precious values that were being destroyed; he was not content to anatomize decay and persisted in believing in the possibility of fresh, healthy growth. In this sense he was an "optimist," and as a writer who believed in "the life of the soul," was dedicated to taking up the challenge of the French novelists by rendering his vision of things in a text as aesthetically "real and visible" as their own.

James repeatedly objected, although on different grounds, to the movement led by Zola. His objection here was not that the work was the product of a limited experience, but that it didn't have roots in experience at all. The new name, "naturalism," did not deceive James for a moment. He believed that novels could be placed only in one of two categories: "that which has life and that which has it not." Usually he had no trouble in placing Zola's work in the latter category. Zola's work was not rooted so much in any actual experience, James felt, as in "experience by imitation." He did not depend upon having impressions, and his ideas were not the result of contemplating direct contacts with life. Too much of his sustenance was drawn from maps, directories, statistical compilations. James thought that, for the artist, there could be no substitute for personal experiences, and to rely upon scientific data was, in his opinion, as dangerous as to rely solely upon the imagination.

Once James asked Zola if he had ever been in Italy. Zola replied that he had been only as far as Genoa, and that had been but a matter of a few days. Later, during the same conversation, Zola revealed to James his plan to write shortly a novel entitled "Rome," extensively treating that city. Such a paradox was a critical revelation for James and in his essay on Zola for *Notes on Novelists* he commented, "It flooded his career, to my sense, with light; it showed how he had marched from subject to subject and had 'got-up' each in turn—showing also how consummately he had reduced such getting-up to an artifice."

Such a crude, mechanical process was a far cry from James's method of proceeding from felt aesthetic perceptions to prolonged contemplation and then to a final, deeply personal expression. He continued his observation on Zola as follows: "But was the adored Rome also to be his on such terms, the Rome he was already giving away before possessing an inch of it? One thought of one's own frequentations, saturations—a history of long years, and of how the effect of them had somehow been but to make the subject too august. Was *he* to find it easy through a visit of a month or two with 'introductions' and a Baedeker?"

James was not blind to the power Zola sometimes achieved and realized that while Zola did not consider man's finer possibilities, he could yet provide, in his promiscuous, collective way, a penetrating and true illustration of "our natural allowance of health, heartiness and grossness." It is true that James was greatly interested in the development of "naturalism" as a literary movement. But whatever scientific truth the work of the "naturalist" writers might have, it had little artistic truth, he believed. Authorities might vouch for the validity of the statistics, charts and so forth, but the final question was did this collection of devices add up to a work of art.

By insisting that the artist should rely as much as possible upon his personal sense of things, James was running counter to the popular current in literary affairs. It was the very absence of a personal quality, the presumed substitution of scientific method for individual capriciousness, that gave much of its authority to "naturalism." This was an old story to James, who had grown up in an atmosphere in which the artist was not considered too reliable a person. Henry James, Sr. thought of art as narrowing and frivolous, and he was disappointed when, in 1860, William decided to be an artist instead of a scientist. The reputation of science was sky-rocketing during James's youth, and knowledge gained from personal experience was considered unreliable as compared with the "true" knowledge of science. Whenever a personal impression conflicted with scientific decree, the impression had to be disregarded. James eventually worked it out that neither the truths of science nor those afforded by personal experience were of much use by themselves. Each had to be considered in terms of the other if they were to be of use to him. But the impressions gained from actual experience, he believed, provided the necessary basis for fruitful thinking and for the creation of satisfactory works of art.

The history of James's ideas on the subject of converting experience into the stuff of art is a protracted one. It is necessary always to bear in mind that his view on such a matter as the aesthetic quality of prose-fiction evolved over several decades. His own creative efforts lagged often considerably to the rear of his critical awareness in this respect as in others. But the view that he held throughout his years as a mature artist and critic was that both the writer and the reader needed strong aesthetic impressions. As James conceived his task, however, this was only part, perhaps even a mere beginning, of the work of art. Both the artist and the reader would have to conduct a prolonged, intensive scrutiny of these sensuous fragments, until they had yielded up every secret they possessed about the workings of the human heart and soul.

2

Experience is never limited, and it is never complete; it is an immense sensibility, a kind of huge spider-web of the finest silken threads suspended in the chamber of consciousness, and catching every air-borne particle in its tissue. It is the very atmosphere of the mind; and when the mind is imaginative—much more when it happens to be that of a man of genius—it takes to itself the faintest hints of life, it converts the very pulses of the air into revelations . . . The power to guess the unseen from the seen, to trace the implications of things, to judge the whole piece by the pattern, the condition of feeling life in general so completely that you are well on your way to knowing any particular corner of it—this cluster of gifts may almost be said to constitute experience, and they occur in country and in town, and in the most differing stages of education. James, The Art of Fiction (1884).

Beyond Appearances

HENRY JAMES COLLECTED IMPRESSIONS IN MUCH THE SAME WAY A small boy might collect bits of shells, oddly shaped stones, pieces of colored glass and so forth, storing them in his pockets and from time to time bringing a treasure out to wonder about it and try to imagine what part it had played in the mysterious world about him. The collected treasure was precious in itself, but equally precious were the possibilities it inspired. Both the treasure and the things imagined were part of the boy's experience, and so they were with Henry James. Perhaps the most remarkable aspect of James's concept of experience is its completely dynamic nature. He takes great care to point out that experience is not any passive reception of impressions. While it is true that impressions may be said to constitute experience,

31

James points out that the power of the mind to examine actively these impressions, to wrest from them all that they have to disclose about life, the very capacity to reflect incisively upon impressions, to seize purposefully the clues which they possess, might also be said to constitute experience.

James demonstrates in this concept the extent to which his thinking was conducted in terms of concrete images. In a way this kind of thinking is similar to that of the metaphysical poets and has earned James the epithet "metaphysical," but his awareness of spiritual reality was far different from theirs. No orthodoxy or dogma had claims upon his intellect; he had at least the illusion of complete freedom to probe each impression with all the hope of discoveries that an explorer might feel on venturing upon unknown regions. His only guides in these investigations were his artistic taste and his moral sense, both of which became keener with the successive accretions of experience. Then, too, if the metaphysical poets were "possessed by death," it may be said that James was possessed by life since all his art was devoted to relishing the impressions it afforded him and penetrating to their deepest meaning. His dissociation from formal religious tradition was not without its penalties; the most terrible and the most serene moments in his art, depending for their strength as they must upon his intensely personal sense of things, were to receive the criticism again and again of being precious.

As a part of their religious instruction, Henry James, Sr. saw to it that his children attended churches of many different faiths. This unusual procedure was supplemented by a good deal of general discussion of religion within the family circle. As a special feature, Henry James, Sr.'s personal theories on religious and philosophical matters frequently supplemented the program. The result of all this exposure was that while Henry

James, Jr. became highly sensitive to the spiritual life, he failed to respond to the claims of any particular church.

This situation did not trouble him deeply. His chief regret in the matter, namely, that he had lost a possible source of impressions, speaks significantly of the extent to which he was devoted to this world, rather than to any possible next. Most of the other children James had associated with were well supplied with visions of hell and heaven, angels, devils, and other spiritual folk, but his family boasted nothing of the sort. To an imagination that fed avidly on aesthetic perceptions, the kind of religious speculation current in his father's works seemed meager fare. James's gentle, generous father was proof enough of the validity of his metaphysical systems, but James could not help occasionally wishing that he might have come across his father at an earlier date, when the father was still dealing with worldly "types of the shepherd and the flock," and would have had something more representational to offer.

Possibly this very absence of an aesthetic concept of the spiritual world incited James to cast about in his impressions for spiritual meanings and to construct artistically an elaborate fusion of image and idea. One of the distinctive characteristics of the metaphysical poets at their best is that they were not only capable of a direct fusion of image and idea, but they were capable of sustaining this image throughout a poem. They could erect an elaborate syllogism in terms of a metaphor, varying its references radically from strophe to strophe, startling the reader with unexpected juxtapositions, and yet maintaining the poem's integrity. However unexpected or complex the sensuous image might be, it had an organic relevance to the rest of the poem.

This fusion of image and idea is also characteristic of James's mature work, and in order to sustain it effectively he needed to have a sense of moral values that operated with clarity and precision, however shadowy its authority. Practically all of the fiction written by James between 1895 and 1904 illustrates that he did have this power. Indeed, certain works such as *The Sacred Fount* illustrate it in excess. There, the manipulation of metaphor is so elaborate that the novel's vitality is drained off, and it becomes an exercise in technique.

The difficulties involved in reconciling shifting concepts of the physical world and of the spiritual world caused the leading thinkers in that corner of America where James grew up to turn almost instinctively to the seventeenth century writers in their efforts to find an articulate expression of their own experience. James's knowledge of seventeenth century literature was evidently slight, but he was well informed on the thought and writing of New Englanders who had given close attention to the writers of the earlier period. His own attention was devoted almost exclusively to nineteenth century writers and to *genres* which concerned his predecessors little. But the awareness of man's inner life which he had acquired to a great extent from his father and his father's circle of friends made him dissatisfied with any literature that did not make some effort to cope with it.

During the 1870's James was to discover tremendous possibilities in the aesthetic technique of the French novelists. But prior to that time there was a decided respect for conscious moralizing apparent in both his fiction and his criticism. It seemed to him that a work of fiction needed to offer these things: first, a dramatic opposition of moral values; second, an analysis of character; and, third, an examination of motive. The primary function of a book, he believed, was to suggest abstract thought. James denounced Trollope for being merely a good observer and accused Dickens of not knowing man, but only men. In his middle twenties, James was a somewhat stern and exacting critic. This was a phase that did not last long; moral values rapidly became conceivable for him only as they exhibited themselves in action, in some aesthetically appreciable form. He came to value the experience which a work of fiction could offer him because of the moral values implicit in the experience.

Since he could not derive any moral enlightenment from most of the work of the French novelists, he characterized the experience afforded by their work as shallow. He believed that they could go no deeper than the epidermis. Actually, such was far from being the case with the writing he denounced on this ground; it was his own inexperience where lower social classes were concerned, as well as with the omnipresent sex motive, that frequently thwarted his perception. For example, the evil that Baudelaire found everywhere in the degraded society about him impressed James as not being "evil," but "nasty." James primly brushed aside Baudelaire's work with the observation that while Baudelaire might have had moral intentions, his choice of subject matter precluded any success. He stared ". . . very hard at a mass of things from which, more intelligently, we avert our heads," was James's ostrich-like conclusion. It must always be borne in mind that James was writing here for a Victorian public; he might have had some private reservations, and he might have somewhat overstated his disapproval so as to reassure his readers.

During the seventies James's experience was greatly enriched in those areas where hitherto it had been somewhat starved. Much of the enrichment came through his personal acquaintance with the French novelists themselves as well as through a fuller understanding of their work. He found that there was often very much to admire in the personalities of these men, and that some of them had performed an incalculable service to the art of fiction. So open did his mind eventually become on the question of "low life" in fiction that, in 1891, he wrote an introduction to Kipling's *Soldiers Three* which included a spirited defense of that writer's choice of subject matter.

When he wrote "The Art of Fiction" in 1884, James was so convinced of the need for dealing with sexual matters in the novel that he took a fresh stand in regard to the condition of English fiction. He now asserted that instead of possessing a moral purpose, it was guilty of a "diffidence." In fact, he said, the English novel's purpose was "rather negative," since it agreed to ignore a large segment of experience.

As James's belief developed that all experience must be considered fit material for art, a corollary belief developed that art should not simply reproduce material as it was found in life, but should deal with it in such a way as to elicit its noble qualities. As early as 1866, in reviewing a translation of Epictetus, James vigorously rejected that aspect of stoicism which indicated that man ought to accept patiently, passively, whatever happened to him. Such stoicism seemed barbaric to James, the philosophy of a mind enslaved. In opposition to the Stoic acceptance of conditions, he held up the Christian faith in a future realization of ideals and a hope that things of the present day could be improved.

Six months after the review of Epictetus, he reviewed Dumas' *Affaire Clemenceau*. While he found it well-written, James was provoked by its unrelieved gloom and its picture of cynicism triumphant to state explicitly what a work of art must do to be great. The declaration, similar to that uttered in the earlier review, gives a clear picture of the artist's moral responsibility in dealing with his material. He wrote, "To be completely great, a work of art must lift up the reader's heart; and it is the artist's secret to reconcile this condition with images of the barest and sternest reality. Life is dispiriting, art is inspiring; and a story-teller who aims at anything more than a fleeting success has no right to tell an ugly story unless he knows its beautiful counterpart. The impression that he should aim to produce on the reader's mind with his work must have much in common with the impression originally produced on his own mind by his subject. If the effect of an efficient knowledge of his subject had been to fill his spirit with melancholy, and to paralyze his better feelings, it would be impossible that his work should be written. Its existence depends on the artist's reaction against the subject; and if the subject is morally hideous, of course this reaction will be in favor of moral beauty."

This statement can easily be misunderstood: James does not say that a writer should ignore material, nor that he should be false to his impressions. James saw the question as basically one of selection and emphasis, and he believed that every artist could so express his material as to confront the reader with an aesthetic presentation of the beautiful and true. Most of the French writers chose to reproduce things as they saw them and, if any moral reaction was in order, to let each reader shift for himself.

James did not have in mind any theory of abstract virtues in accordance with which the appearance of things was to be judged. The "ideal world" which he projected in his fiction was one constructed out of images that had been directly perceived by his senses. It was a world that was involved in constant interaction with the actual world as he perceived it. If he received an impression of spiritual ugliness, it was absorbed into his experience, where, through the action of imagination and will, it was made to reveal its counterpart in spiritual beauty. It is more correct here to speak of an "idealizing process" than of an "ideal world." This would describe more accurately the dynamic nature of James's vision of the ideal and its condition of working only with aesthetic perceptions of the everyday world.

If the writing of fiction was for James an "act of life," it was also an "act of faith." The sensitive, thoughtful figures that he set in motion again and again in his writing are an active expression of his belief that the world could be improved. His novels are a kind of dramatized philosophy, representing a sensitive examination of life, reflecting clashes of social values and historical tendencies, and projecting the possibility of a finer order of experience. James was well aware of the danger inherent in his method, that the experience his work offered might appear so unreal as to be considered merely "romance." To prevent this he tried to make his work conform as closely as possible to the actual conditions of life. When he looked back over his work with a view to writing prefaces for a collected edition, he considered that he had been on the whole successful in maintaining an illusion of life. The most notable exception, he felt, was in his causing the Bellegardes to act nobly in *The American*. A better knowledge of the French aristocracy had convinced him that instead of rejecting the wealthy Newman, they would have swallowed him whole.

The pitfall ready and waiting for a critic with James's high-mindedness was not only the undervaluation of novels such as those written by the French novelists, but the overvaluation of novels that were heavily philosophic. The history of James's opinions on George Sand is the history of his scramble out of such a pitfall. When he was a reviewer during the late 1860's he lavished admiration upon the "philosophic" element in George Sand's fiction. His admiration included the flattery of imitation. James was by no means alone in this high opinion of George Sand, for she held a very high position in the general

American critical esteem. Her romances were considered to reflect the finest sentiment and the noblest conduct. Walt Whitman elected her Consuelo as his favorite heroine in literature, and Hawthorne, seeking to communicate the poetic and transcendental flavor of his hero, Miles Coverdale, made him an interminable reader of Emerson's *Essays, The Dial,* Carlyle, and George Sand. In 1851, George Sand prefixed a "Notice" to her *La Petite Fadette* to counsel her public that, "In times when the evil lies in that men misunderstand and hate one another, it is the artist's mission to celebrate gentleness, confidence, friendship, and thus to remind hardened or discouraged men that pure manners, tender sentiments, and primitive equity do, or could still exist in the world." This mission, as she accomplished it in her romances, is what first attracted James to George Sand.

The tide had commenced to turn by 1877 when James observed once more that George Sand had style and was "nothing if not philosophic," but pointed out that her work had no form. In addition, he pointed out, she was a sentimentalist, not a moralist; she perceived, but rarely judged—hence her books had wisdom but no weight. At this time the significant aspect of James's interest in George Sand is his concern with her ability to convert her experience into art. Making acquaintance with life at first hand, he declared, was the great thing that Madame Sand, as a woman, achieved.

The publication in the *Revue de Paris* (November 1, 1896) of letters sent by George Sand to Alfred de Musset led James to reflect at length upon the extraordinary gift she had of converting an experience made up so much of quarrels, unfortunate love affairs, and other graceless facts into luminous and charming works of art. No matter how rough the grain that came to her mill, it was all turned into flour of the smoothest texture. James observed that like the great male lovers of that romantic age, Goethe, Byron, Napoleon, she had lived through a succession of amours. "If millions of women, of course, of every condition, had had more lovers," James wrote, "it was probable that no woman independently so occupied and so diligent had had, as might be said, more unions." Somehow, out of the wreckage of each affair, something was salvaged for her art. She, herself, rose phoenix-like from the successive consuming fires, ". . . withal only the more just and bright and true, the more sane and superior, improved and improving."

James attached considerable importance to the idea that an artist should seize upon whatever impressions life afforded him. To delay in the hope that some ideally suitable impression might drift into one's reach was to court failure. One of James's earliest short stories, *The Madonna of the Future,* had depicted the misfortunes of a painter who was too obsessed with an ideal to commence work on the material that lay to hand. One of James's latest stories, *The Beast in the Jungle,* dealt with a similar theme, in that its protagonist failed to find the items of experience that came to him good enough for him to appropriate them. In both instances experience revenged itself upon the protagonists, leaving their lives sterile and desolate. The opposite of these two stories is the story of George Sand's life, as James considered it.

The labor of creating a work of art was always a labor of love with James, and he felt that such was the way it should be. Art was, for him, a kind of religion that had its promises and its guarantees for faithful service. That is why Flaubert's agonized struggle with words puzzled and dismayed James. He recognized that such was often the case, but wondered why it should be so. When a fresh volume of Karenine's biography of George Sand appeared and reminded James once more of her extraordinary career, he exclaimed, "That is what it is really to *have* style—when you set about performing the act of life." Again he mused on her ability to make her experience, however agitated and spotted it might be, serve the purposes of a style pure and serene, and he pointed the pragmatic moral, "What this felicity most comes to in fact is that doing at any cost the work that lies to one's hand shines out again and yet again as the saving secret of the soul."

James had commenced by admiring George Sand as a "philosophic" writer and had finished by admiring, not nearly so much the quality of her philosophic thought, as her ability to convert her dubious adventures into charming and edifying prose. This development of James's moral sense and his sense of the relationship between experience and art is more dramatically illustrated in the history of his attitude towards George Eliot. Here, again, he had begun by praising the novelist as a philosophical novelist. There were faults to be found in her artistry, but James admired her sympathetic treatment of character in its outward as well as inward appearance. Her work seemed a splendid illustration of the reward that could come from a close scrutiny of environment.

George Eliot had an explicit moral purpose in writing her novels. She wanted to communicate her own views, but she also wanted to raise the level of contemporary fiction. She immediately found a public entirely in sympathy with her aims and was highly successful. The American literary circles were especially pleased with the moral tone of her work. As her reputation increased, so did the scope of her novels and the burden of philosophy which they were forced to carry.

Instead of being pleased by this turn of events, James grew progressively more dismayed by the use to which George Eliot was putting her great talent. The strength and charm that attached to her early works, which were based almost wholly on her close observation of people and places, were partially dissipated in *Middlemarch* and *Daniel Deronda,* it seemed to him, by a mist of philosophic and idealizing reflection. It was evident to James that many of the characters in these novels were for the most part based on invention rather than observation, and whenever invention played a large part she had achieved at best a brilliant failure.

It was James's opinion that George Eliot was the victim of her age. This observation is significant not only as it bears upon George Eliot, but also in that it gives evidence of James's sense of the temper of the times in which he lived. One of the reasons George Eliot's career fascinated James must have been that the course she charted would have been such an easy course for him to follow. He sensed, too, that George Eliot had his predilection for aesthetic expression, that she was not naturally a philosopher, a "critic of the universe," but preferred to observe life and feel it deeply. She chose, however, to write for her age. This brought success and the approval of the critics she most respected. To James her example was an instructive warning.

The moralizing and philosophizing which gave George Eliot fame in her day have since caused her to be one of the least read of the important nineteenth century writers. The tendency of the age to dissociate sense from sensibility proved, as James suggests, her downfall. The decline of faith in that period must have seemed to James to be having strange consequences for the novel: in France there was a paramount concern with sense impressions and a disregard of moral values; in England, as adjudged by the work of George Eliot, the concern with morals tended to sacrifice all but a minimum regard for the senses. To paraphrase a remark from another context, in France the novel was losing its mind, in England it was losing its senses.

James's final view of George Eliot reflects the importance he attached to dealing with ideas only through aesthetic perceptions that were drawn from actual impressions. George Eliot had let reflection play too great a role at the expense of direct sense perception, so that while her characters were "deeply studied and massively supported," they were not "*seen*." She had allowed "culture" to make up her mind on a great many subjects, rather than submit her judgment to "the more primitive processes of experience." James considered *Romola* to be the finest thing George Eliot wrote, but what he singled out as its chief defect was, in the last analysis, the same defect that blighted much of Zola's work. She had relied too much on documentation, on learning, to evoke a sense of the city of her story. A fragment of her erudition would have sufficed for James, if only he could have felt the breath of the Florentine streets, seen their colors, smelled their odors, and heard their sounds.

A third writer, Ivan Turgenieff, must be considered in connection with the development of James's concept of how an artist must deal first of all with his sense impressions, must derive his moral ideas from these impressions and express them aesthetically in his art. Turgenieff, both the man and his works, had more influence on James in this connection than did any other writer or body of writings during the decade following James's permanent move to Europe in 1875. Prior to this period, James had admired Turgenieff but with reservations. His desire to see displayed in fiction a concern for "pure manners, tender sentiments," and so forth was precisely what dampened his first enthusiasm for the Russian novelist. Unlike George Sand, who after all differed only in degree from other romancers, and George Eliot, who was associated with a broad literary and philosophic tradition, Turgenieff was a unique case that excited and troubled James. He was a member of Flaubert's circle, yet he was completely apart from that group through his "apprehension of man's religious impulses, of the *ascetic* passion . . ." There was a humility about Turgenieff's work that was more than welcome to James after exposure to Balzac's blatant pretensions to be the great showman of the human comedy. If, like the French realists, Turgenieff showed "an excessive attention to detail," the young reviewer was willing to pardon this since Turgenieff's attention was always directed to the *"morally interesting."*

What Turgenieff saw of life and what he put into his writing had a deeply melancholy cast. His finest work expressed the misery of the great mass of his fellow-Russians. Of the unrelieved grimness and hopelessness in Turgenieff's account, James did not wholly approve. He was not looking for anything so naive as a happy ending or so false as a rosy tint applied to somber truths. He did, however, feel that Turgenieff had merely warmed over reality and served it up without attempting to spice the dish with some glimpse of happy possibilities. James accused Turgenieff of being no better than a pessimist, and observed, "We value most the 'realists' who have an ideal of delicacy and the elegiasts who have an ideal of joy." In 1875, a year after making this criticism, an important enlargement of experience came to James in the nature of a personal acquaintance with Turgenieff; it swept away all of his misgivings.

James found himself admiring everything about the Russian novelist—his appearance, his conversation, his whole personality. That Turgenieff apparently cared little for James's literary efforts did not deter the latter. The remarks he made about Turgenieff in his letters home glowed with praise. The two spent many hours together discussing literature—at cafés, at Tur-

genieff's apartment atop Montmartre, and on Sunday afternoons when Turgenieff took James along to the Flaubert gatherings. When James wrote about Turgenieff in 1884, shortly
after his death, James's deep personal fondness for the man
pervaded the sketch. He sensed that Turgenieff was "of the
stuff of which glories are made," and that his fictions and dramas
were only a part of the greater drama of his life—the struggle
for a better way of life in Russia.

Some of James's observations on Turgenieff in his "partial
portrait" can be applied closely to his own development at the
time. For example, he notes that Turgenieff "had so the habit
of observation, that he perceived in excruciating sensations all
sorts of curious images and analogies." James made particular
note of the fact that Turgenieff did not rest content with appearances, as did the French writers. "He had his reservations
and discriminations, and he had, above all, the great back-
garden of his Slav imagination and his Germanic culture, into
which the door constantly stood open, and the grandsons of
Balzac were not, I think, particularly free to accompany him."

James, similarly, had his reservations and discriminations,
and he had earlier taken the French novelists to task for refus-
ing to give English culture and literary tradition, let alone
American, consideration in their discussions of art. Like James,
Turgenieff was not concerned with plots, but preferred his
stories to grow out of some impression, usually an impression
centering in one or more individuals. Similar impressions of
actual persons were becoming of prime importance for James's
work and he used the name *disponibles* to describe them.

But aside from any influence directly bearing upon their
mutual craft of writing, Turgenieff had the more fundamental
value for James of broadening and deepening his social hori-
zons. Turgenieff had an enormous capacity for friendship, and

his friends were drawn from all classes and from most of the countries of Europe. He was familiar, through direct contact, with the standards and conventions of a great many local cultures. His personal culture was firmly rooted and liberal enough to permit him to dwell with local gods and yet remain free of their power. In the company of Turgenieff, James felt his own outlook shrink into a surprisingly narrow perspective: "He felt and understood the opposite sides of life; he was imaginative, speculative, anything but literal. . . . Our Anglo-Saxon, Protestant, moralistic, conventional standards were far away from him, and he judged things with a freedom and spontaneity in which I found a perpetual refreshment."

After such knowledge of Turgenieff, the failure to respond to experience with a more humane tolerance and understanding would have been unforgivable indeed.

James came to consider it one of the greatest blessings of art that it could make him intimate with experience that otherwise he could never hope to know. The more remote the experience was from his own, the more he was apt to value it. Because he wanted so very much to enlarge his own experience by adding to it the experience of men whose viewpoint was utterly different from his own, he insisted firmly that the new writers rising to prominence in England should express their *personal* vision of things. When James inveighed against the formlessness of the work of these new novelists, it was because the lack of treatment, of concern with what was essentially interesting in their material, prevented him from sitting at the window of another man's consciousness. Amongst the new writers James found Joseph Conrad far and away the most gifted in this matter of expressing a unique view of experience; his work was always the result of painstaking artistry and an unrelenting concern with the true source of interest in his material.

By and large James considered the variety of experience being poured out to the English reading public by such writers as H. G. Wells, Arnold Bennett, Compton Mackenzie, and D. H. Lawrence to be a decidedly healthy thing, particularly after the cloying effect on English letters of the "art for art's sake" movement. James was completely out of sympathy with that phenomenon. He had inevitably come in contact with some of its leaders, and this only strengthened his resolve to remain free from any connection with them. His dislike for Oscar Wilde was not at all mitigated by the fact that Wilde's brittle comedies were playing to packed theaters while James's cherished offspring, *Guy Domville,* died a-borning. When his stories were to appear in the *Yellow Book,* James writhed at the prospect of their being illustrated by Beardsley.

This reaction against the devotees of "art for art's sake" in England brings into clearer relief James's conviction that art must develop from the artist's personal impressions of life and from an attempt to grasp any implications for life as a whole that may be latent in these impressions. While many of the artists enrolled under the "art for art's sake" banner believed themselves devoted beyond all else to a closer apprehension of life, James found it to be seldom so in practice. It was generally a pretension, rather than a fact.

Not long after taking up his residence in England, James published *A Bundle of Letters* (1879). This short-story satirized the "aesthetes," who had experienced so little of the life they made such a fuss about. Louis Leverett, a young man from Boston, goes to Paris in search of "Life." His letter to Harvard Tremont, a friend who has not yet shed the hair-shirt of Boston, is replete with the era's clichés. He frequently jumbles the remarks of Pater, Ruskin, and Swinburne. Louis exclaims, " 'The great thing is to *live,* you know—to feel, to be conscious of one's possibilities; not to pass through life mechanically and insensibly, even as a letter through the post-office.' " He trusts he has not shocked his correspondent and dwells fondly upon his artistic temperament. " 'And in Boston one can't live—*on ne peut pas vivre,* as they say here.' "

Many of the expressions which James places on the lips of Louis Leverett, such as the exhortations "to live," and "to feel," are the same ones he employed in his own discussions of art. The vital difference was that James qualified his terms to mean far more than simply variety of sensation and sensation for its own sake. By "to live" and "to feel" James meant for the artist to be ever alert to the sensuous impressions life afforded him, but also to force these impressions to open as a window upon a perspective of character and yield a deeper understanding of human nature, of social conditions, of spiritual elements functioning in human behavior. Life in its sensuous aspects was important, but far more so when these aspects yielded significant meanings. For the Louis Leveretts of the period, "art for art's sake" was largely an excuse for trifling with art. James pointed out that they really understood their masters rather poorly. He has Louis Leverett exclaim, " 'That's the great thing—to be free, to be frank, to be naïf,' " and then loftily attribute the remark to Arnold, Swinburne or Pater. Louis further observes, " '. . . art should never be didactic and what's life but the finest of arts? Pater has said that so well somewhere. . . .' "

James had written in *Benvolio* (1875), "Curiosity for curiosity's sake, art for art's sake, these were essentially broken-winded steeds. Ennui was at the end of everything that did not multiply our relations with life." The revival of taste, a sense of beauty, the general aesthetic renascence which seemed, to the Louis Leveretts, to be at hand in England was a broken-winded steed for James because it persisted in looking at life through "culture." It was, at bottom, an effort to escape experience.

The Pre-Raphaelite movement was a case in point. William James wrote to Henry in 1883, "You ought to have seen the Rossetti exhibition,—the work of a boarding-school girl, no color, no drawing, no cleverness of any sort, nothing but feebleness incarnate, and a sort of refined intention of an extremely narrow sort, with no technical power to carry it out."

Henry responded with hearty agreement, adding that it was one of the reasons why, if it was good to have one foot in England, it was better, "or at least as good, to have the other out of it." Pre-Raphaelite painting was, for James, an example of the results obtained when the artist lives off the artistic products of others, without a consideration of the human conditions through which they were conceived, or without a sense of an affinity between such artistic products and the conditions of his own experience.

The effect of such a movement as Pre-Raphaelitism was to turn the attention of its devotee away from any sensitive examination of the world about him. Instead of multiplying his relations with life, or even with works of art that clarified and rendered explicit the forces affecting his life, art became a dead end, beginning and ending with itself. James considered it so important "to live" in the sense in which he employed the term, that he placed such an appeal at the heart of *The Ambassadors,* where Lambert Strether makes his famous plea, beginning "Live all you can . . ." to the young American artist, Little Bilham.

James's practice of "art for art's sake" was an effort to live as intensely as possible by realizing his impressions through expressing them in the form of art. Art was for him, it must be remembered, an "act of life." He did not work at his art, as so many other writers of the period did, for the sake of morality, or religion, or social reform, or simply for entertainment. He worked at it because the very creative process yielded him a fine and rare order of experience and, too, because it made this order of experience available to others.

In a sense, then, while James did not propagandize for any specific moral or social reform, he may be said to be always conducting a campaign to raise the general level of human experience. For what are his Fledas, Millies, Isabels, but persons dedicated to finer experience, casting an ironic shadow, as they move, on a pretentious and vain actuality? Lambert Strether and his kind project the ideal case in dynamic interaction with familiar realities. Their presence offers a counterpoise to the vulgarity and evil which is omnipresent in the world. James was no optimist, in the usual sense of the word, and the grim conditions that can afflict the human spirit become very real in his pages, but he was also no pessimist. In his hands, even so fragile and finite a creature as Maisie of *What Maisie Knew* can bring about a convincing transfiguration amidst sordid actualities and characters as cynical and disabused as any to appear in the work of those writers who pretend to offer "a slice of life."

The true thing that most matters to us is the true thing we have the most use for, and there are surely many occasions on which the truest thing of all is the necessity of the mind, its simple necessity of feeling. Whether it feels in order to learn or learns in order to feel, the event is the same: the side on which it shall most feel will be the side to which it will most incline. James, Notes on Novelists, "George Sand, 1897."

Felt Experience

THE HOUSEHOLD IN WHICH HENRY JAMES GREW UP WAS CERTAINLY one of the most intellectual in America. Henry James, Sr. was an exceedingly likeable person, and he had an enthusiasm for exploring philosophic and religious matters that led him to seek out the people whose ideas interested him and to invite them to spend some time in his family circle. When prominent European literary figures visited the United States, they were more than apt to make the James residence a port of call. The family traveled a great deal and had many friends both in Europe and America. As a result, the James children grew up in an atmosphere rich with ideas and were alive to many of the important questions of the day; they were personally familiar with some of the men who were leaders of contemporary thought.

It seems paradoxical, in view of all this traffic with ideas and intellectuals, that Henry James should emerge as a man who disdained to think in abstract terms, and that William James should have been one of the most influential leaders of anti-intellectualism. Yet, amid such a free exchange of ideas, such tolerance of opinion, such exposure to different possibilities for belief, and such freedom from any pressure to accept and conform, it is perhaps only to be expected that William and Henry should have preferred to keep free of any formalized beliefs and established positions. Their constantly shifting perspective of social and religious forms would have made the intrusion of any one form into their lives ridiculous.

A fundamental tenet of the Pragmatism which William James was to champion held that it was impossible to dissociate emotions, or what is generally understood as "feeling," from an individual's thought. This was opposed to the intellectualists' view that in order to know purely, it was necessary to eliminate any personal or subjective elements that might color thought. In the best intellectualist tradition, a scholar or a critic, would judge his subject-matter only with reference to general criteria, verifiable facts, established laws, and would ignore any personal feelings that might attempt to influence his thinking.

The Pragmatist view, however, regarded man as an organism in constant interaction with his environment, using thought only as a means of bettering his relation to his environment. To William James, it seemed that the mental life was never so rich as at the moment when it registered direct sensuous impressions. As a philosopher he had to deal constantly with logic and ideological abstractions. This never ceased to irk him, and the test he devised for any theoretical proposition was to try to see how it would actually work in practice. At times William James regretted that he had not stuck to painting, and he envied people like his brother Henry "to whom aesthetic revelations of things were the real world."

It is pertinent to cite William James's views here on the importance of feeling and of sensuous impressions because they parallel very closely the views of Henry. The latter, however, would never divorce thought from feeling and consequently diverged from the idea held by William that sheer "feeling" was to be reckoned as a good and that the terminus of thought was action. Henry James's view of the activist principle in *Pragmatism* was much closer to that of his friend Charles S. Peirce (with whom he frequently dined during the winter of 1875-76 in Paris), who held that the end of thought is action only in so far as the end of the action is another thought.

Although Henry James tried to keep up with his brother's publications and their correspondence often touched on philosophical matters, philosophy *per se* did not interest him. His concern with the importance of feeling and its relation to thought was limited to the field of art, and he arrived at his opinions largely through examination of his own experience. His early opinions, apparent in the reviews he published from 1864 to 1866, indicate that he took considerable pains to conceal any element of personal feeling in his writing and to maintain a tone that was coolly rational and intellectual. He even adopted a smug superiority in grinding under his heel so exuberant a display of personal feeling as Whitman's *Drum-taps*. Mild-mannered Trollope received several tart reprimands from James, and in a review dealing with Edmond Scherer he observed that the critic is "in the nature of his function opposed to his author."

James seems to speak in these early reviews with fixed ideas as to what a novelist should or should not do. He is not hesitant to make his point. There is, generally speaking, an absence of the personal note and of the inclination to approach sympathetically the works reviewed. Much of this may have been due to the attitude of James's publishers, who were earnestly concerned with improving the quality of American literature and refining the public's taste. Also, with his own creative aspirations in mind, James was an avid student of literary technique and apt to deal abruptly with whatever struck him as poor workmanship.

Some of the qualities that James admired very much in the

novels he was reading at this time were what might be termed "philosophic sweep," the tendency to moralize and a certain tone of sad seriousness. Excessive passion disturbed him, and he took a Mrs. Seemuller to task because she permitted her characters to be motivated by their instincts rather than their reason. James tried to achieve these qualities in his own first short stories and, for better or for worse, enjoyed some success at it. *The Story of a Year*, written when he was twenty-one, is almost entirely given over to analysis of the states of mind of the heroine. Lizzie Crowe acts from misplaced "affections," but James has so convinced his reader that she is shallow, and her temptations are so persuasive, that little case is made for morality. While stories such as *My Friend Bingham* (1867) and *Poor Richard* (1867) might have had some basis in James's experience they give little evidence of personal feeling on the part of the author and a good deal of evidence that he was trying to capture the air of sweet reasonableness he admired in the work of others.

Neither James's criticism nor his fiction began to show much promise until he commenced to place more confidence in his own impressions, and his broadening experience freed him from too heavy a dependence upon literary models. His criticism discloses an increasing dissatisfaction with pre-conceived rules and fixed ideas. The shift in James's attitude towards certain critics and with regard to the functions of criticism stems directly from his growing belief in the fundamental importance of an individual's capacity to feel. At the start of his career, James was highly suspicious of any marked evidence of personal feeling in a critic's work, but a decade or so later it was this quality of a personal, felt response that determined for him the whole question of a critic's worth.

James almost made an exception to his fixed ideas in the case of Matthew Arnold when he reviewed that writer's *Essays in*

Criticism in 1865. He could not help but praise Arnold's sensitive grasp of literature, and yet it was evident that a deep, personal feeling for specific works of literature guided Arnold's judgments. Here was evidence of strong feeling on literary matters interacting with a powerful mind. Was Arnold right in letting his feelings influence matters, James wondered. Surely, he reflected, it is reason, entirely disconnected from feeling, that determines the best criticism. He juggled the question uncertainly; there was something to be said for both sides.

"It is hard to say whether the literary critic is more called upon to understand or to feel. It is certain that he will accomplish little unless he can feel acutely; although it is perhaps equally certain that he will become weak the moment he begins to 'work,' as we may say, his natural sensibilities. The best critic is probably he who leaves his feelings out of account, and relies upon reason for success." Thus, the first round went to reason.

If the work of critics who relied on their feelings was suspect, it followed that little could be expected by way of valuable opinion from non-professionals whose reactions were almost invariably conditioned by their emotions. If the public was to be educated at all, it at least had to be supplied with critical opinions that were based purely on reason, James decided. It is plain in all this that James believed some abstract method could be applied by intelligent men to literature much as scientific techniques were applied in a qualitative analysis of matter. The intrusion of human feeling in either case would only admit the possibility of error.

This discussion of James's attitude toward Arnold indicates James's early position on the relation of feeling to criticism. How his position altered can be seen reflected in his discussion of two French critics, Scherer and Sainte-Beuve. Three months after publication of his review on Arnold, a review appeared in which James discussed the work of these men. Scherer had stated flatly in the preface to his literary studies that his book had no doctrines. He had proceeded entirely in accordance with his feelings, regardless of inconsistencies or contradictions. Nevertheless, he observed that there was a certain firm unity in a man's feelings, which developed by a strictly logical process. In the absence of doctrines, then, there was always "a certain irrepressible moral substance." James questioned whether Scherer's want of doctrines was a merit, but he was willing to pass over this point in order to rejoice in the idea of a critic operating upon a basis of moral unity. This was certainly the ideal critic, "content neither to reason on matters of feeling nor to sentimentalize on matters of reason, equitable, dispassionate, sympathetic."

The second half of this review was devoted to an attack on Sainte-Beuve. James stated his preference for Scherer over Sainte-Beuve because of the positive morality in the former. What Scherer had referred to as his "feelings," was now referred to by James as "moral unity," and "conscience." At this time, there would have been little doubt in James's mind but that the dictates of conscience, assuming always the conscience was that of a "gentleman," and the dictates of reason would go hand in hand.

A little over ten years later, when James reviewed Scherer's *Literary Studies,* he no longer viewed reason, feeling, and morality as distinctly separable elements. He was well on the way to considering the first two as interfused components of the process of perception and reflection. Morality was now by no means objective and absolute, but a relative and subjective sense of things, heavily dependent upon personal experience. Scherer's "moral unity" was, at this stage of James's development, of far less consequence than the narrow range of interest, the "odd lapses and perversities of taste," which James now noted in his work. Sainte-Beuve, on the other hand, had risen highly in James's esteem. Freedom from critical dogma, intelligent and sensitive discriminations, an extensive range of appreciation, a distinctive personal quality—these were the characteristics of a critic that now impressed James. He had spoken before of Sainte-Beuve's passion for literature. In a study of Sainte-Beuve published in 1880, James remarked that the French critic had "two passions which are commonly assumed to exclude each other—the passion for scholarship and the passion for life." Aside from poets and novelists, James asserted that Sainte-Beuve was the writer who had succeeded in introducing into literature the "largest element of life."

The changes in James's critical method during the 'seventies and 'eighties reflect his changing opinion of the role of the critic and, more basically, of the importance of felt experience. The studies collected under the title *French Poets and Novelists* (1878) and the ones which followed display his increasing tendency to rely upon his personal feelings in regard to a work or an author, as well as an increasing tolerance for the methods of different schools and individuals. The studies in *Partial Portraits* (1888) have all a highly "Jamesian" flavor, and some of them, for example those on Turgenieff and duMaurier, depend almost exclusively upon his personal reminiscence for their strength. James came to believe that the highest qualification a critic could have was a capacity for intense emotional response. He wrote, in "The Science of Criticism" (1893) that the critic is pledged, "To lend himself, to project himself, to feel and feel till he understands, and to understand so well that he can say, to have perception at the pitch of passion and expression as embracing as the air, to be infinitely curious and incorrigibly patient, and yet plastic and inflammable and determinable, stooping to conquer, and serving to direct—these are fine chances for an active mind, chances to add the idea of independent beauty to the conception of success. Just in proportion as he is sentient and restless, just in proportion as he reacts and reciprocates and penetrates, is the critic a valuable instrument; for in literature assuredly criticism *is* the critic, just as art is the artist; it being assuredly the artist who invented art and the critic who invented criticism, and not the other way round."

This description of what is required of the critic goes far beyond the advice to give up theories and rules about art. It suggests a complete submission of the self to the conditions of the work of art, being prepared to receive positively whatever it may offer, and being willing to pursue with patience and vigor its obscure and difficult courses. After the critic has had his experience, he is free to have his say, to praise or blame as the case might be.

To possess the capacity to be a great critic in James's sense of the term, was to be able to live more intensely, more perceptively than other men. James's plea for "Criticism, for Discrimination, for Appreciation," applied to life as well as to literature, and the practice of critical analysis of works of art, he believed, made the mind more sharply aware of all experience, not merely that afforded by art. Real criticism, he maintained, is "the very education of our imaginative life," and not only nourishes it, but safeguards it from the merely instinctual, the automatic, and the stupid.

The felt relation to experience which James gradually came to believe was so necessary for a critic, he considered even more obligatory for a writer of fiction. Even at the time of his early reviews, when he was very suspicious of any display of feeling on the critic's part, he considered that some emotional involvement with his subject was necessary for the creative artist. For example, he praised the way in which Mrs. Gaskell dealt with "her affections, her feelings, her associations," although he found it surprising that she had achieved so much success with such "a minimum of head." James also took Victor Hugo to task for neglecting the "heart" in *Les Travailleurs de la Mer.* "... We believe it to have been written exclusively from the head," James stated. "This fact we deeply regret, for we have an enormous respect for M. Victor Hugo's heart." James use of "heart" and "head" in these reviews suggests the critical terminology popular a century earlier; it suggests, also, the generally held belief that reason and emotion were separable elements in a work of fiction.

For a perspective of James's increasing valuation of felt experience in the novel, it is best to turn to his successive estimates of Anthony Trollope. James reviewed Trollope more than he reviewed any other novelist during the period from 1864-66, and although he found some of Trollope's stories pleasing, he did so with condescension. All in all, Trollope struck James as employing very little "head." *Linda Tressel* (1868) was not markedly different from the novels by Trollope that James had previously reviewed, but his reception of it reveals a greater warmth and less insistence upon its being what it was not. Trollope had once more cultivated his little patch of human life, adding nothing, but taking nothing away, and James seemed for once content that it should be so. The process of mellowing had begun, and by 1883, when James came to write the study of Trollope included in *Partial Portraits*, it was complete.

The opening sentence of that study identified Trollope with "that group of admirable writers who, in England, during the preceding half century, had done so much to elevate the art of the novelist." Instead of his former exasperation at Trollope's failure to exercise more intellect in coping with his material, James isolated Trollope's peculiar genius as his "complete appreciation of the usual." Trollope's strength lay in that ". . . he *felt* all daily and immediate things as well as saw them; felt them in a simple, direct, salubrious way, with their sadness, their gladness, their charm, their comicality, all their obvious and measurable meanings."

This, James recognized, led to a far more precise and sensitive knowledge of experience than could be obtained through the intelligence. Trollope didn't need to resort to a conscious analysis of his character's motives or deliberate on their actions, because he "felt their feelings and struck the right note, because he had, as it were, a good ear."

While the evolution of James's views on felt experience worked in Trollope's favor, the same might not be said for most English novelists. James came to consider them notoriously deficient in the matter of feeling. Their whole relation to life seemed far too hampered by rules, insulated by habit, and inhibited by the spirit of an age which inclined to look with favor upon the suppression of the life of the senses. Their concept of the novel reflected these conditions, to its disgrace. Publishers and editors were apt to reject anything that did not seem like proper fare for a reading public of virgins at "the awkward age."

There were many writers in England, of course, who had responded with deep feeling to experience and had managed to communicate a sense of this relationship in their art. James pointed out that while Stevenson did not feel everything equally, "his feelings are always his reasons." "He regards them, whatever they may be, as sufficiently honourable, does not disguise them in other names or colours, and looks at whatever he meets in the brilliant candle-light that they shed."

Always conceding, then, certain important exceptions, James was nevertheless finally of the opinion that Anglo-Saxons were inclined to discount the value of "reactions of sensibility." He was also quite at a loss to account for this, especially as sensibility could be expected to lay few traps for "a race to which the very imagination of it may be said, I think, to have been comparatively denied."

There was no lack of feeling, James recognized, in the fiction being produced in France and Italy. Rather, the danger in these countries was more likely to be that of a wanton exploitation of feeling. Still, it is in connection with two great French novelists, Zola and George Sand, that a further aspect of James's concept of the relation of feeling to experience, and the consequences of this relationship for art, emerge most clearly. This aspect concerns the part feeling plays in regard to truth.

Zola represented for James the archetype of the writer who tries to secure an air of truth for his works by building them upon elaborate documentation. Zola was so convinced of the ability of statistics, maps, photographs and similar material to communicate truth that he proceeded to turn over to the public practically every fact he could lay his hands on and even included all the details of a searching examination of his body made by a physician. James questioned the success of this method. He maintained that he would have understood Zola better without all the particulars on the latter's digestive tract and sense of smell. It seemed to James that details such as these and the countless other more or less sordid details that Zola and his followers gratuitously strewed in the path of their readers discouraged feeling, or at best misdirected it. Underlying James's attitude is his belief that our needs direct our concern with truth, that feeling is often the greatest necessity for understanding, and that thought will go in the direction of the strongest feeling. For artists to picture society as so many rats in a hole struck James as a poor way to go about promoting a sympathetic understanding of human conditions. Too often James saw novels exploiting social horrors, saw the experience of art degenerated to an affair of cheap thrills and all its constructive potentialities sacrificed.

In the fiction of his "major phase" James tried to put felt experience ideally to use. He never meant to postulate feeling as an end in itself. Feeling goes hand in hand with thinking, and the result of their operation is a continuum of impressions through which an individual's experience evolves. This process makes it possible for an artist to direct feeling so as to achieve certain goals. The reader for whom *The Wings of the Dove,* or *The Ambassadors,* or *The Golden Bowl* has been a felt experience has an understanding of certain phases of life that no number of documents could give him.

James's last study of George Sand expressed the view that because of the immense amount of feeling that had gone into her work, it had a certain moral truth and was of value to her readers as a criticism of life. James had no illusions about George Sand's moral anchorage. He had written in 1877 that "her religious feeling, like all her feelings, was powerful and voluminous, and she had an ideal of a sort of etherealized and liberated Christianity, in which unmarried but affectionate couples might find an element friendly to their expansion." But while the group that gathered at Nohant may have been abandoned to emotional excess for its own sake, George Sand kept a firm hold on her moral sense and her philosophic habit. James supposed that any prolonged association with her must have afforded high moral advantages and an education of the soul.

James's last appreciation of George Sand, written in 1914,

reconciles her deeply emotional nature with her moral nobility. It is a kind of culminating affirmation of James's belief in the value of feeling, not only for art, but for what it could do for the imagination, for the expansion of interests and sympathies, and by way of vitalizing culture. His youthful adulation of George Sand had been irrational, quite against what he understood to be his "better sense." His last generous praise of her life and work indicates how thoroughly he enjoyed the freedom from "Anglo-Saxon, Protestant, moralistic, conventional standards" that he had recognized as Turgenieff's freedom. To admire, questions of form aside, a "grand final rightness," a "*general* humanity" in George Sand, a moral integrity out of reach of prejudice, was indeed to have flown beyond the nets.

4

To feel a unity, a character and a tone in one's impressions, to feel them related and all harmoniously coloured, that was positively to face the aesthetic, the creative, even quite wondrously, the critical life and almost on the spot to commence author. James, Notes of a Son and Brother, *1914.*

The Role of Feeling

IN *Notes of a Son and Brother,* HENRY JAMES DESCRIBES HIS youth, made up of so many fruitful years in Europe, as well as in New York, Cambridge, and Newport. He records that he was at this stage aware of impressions gathering in his mind that seemed to demand expression. Still there was as yet no principle which organized these impressions into an inspiration for art. They crowded upon one another and each seemed worth reproducing in its own right, but no relationship assimilated any large group of them into a whole.

Before he could use his impressions, James had to feel unifying themes linking them together. This he did at a very early stage in his career, and his subsequent work developed with increasing subtlety and beauty variations on these original themes. Eventually, to judge from his notebooks, the process of creative expression became for James a time during which he yielded himself up completely to the aesthetic situations projected by his imagination. At such times he lived intensely, meditating with prolonged and careful attention upon the characters and scenes he imagined, above all exploring the way he felt about them. To enter this world of imagination was to leave the world of the habitual and commonplace, to explore beyond appearances, to inquire with leisure and freedom into relations, motivations, general conditions. The passage into this imaginative life, "the world of creation," had a compelling charm for him. In the privacy of his notebooks he speaks of it

64

at times as though it were a kind of Xanadu looming in his dreams.

James's vital need to live in the world of creation arose, not from a desire to escape from actuality, but from a desire to penetrate deeply into its mysteries. Life, it seemed to James, bungled its affairs badly. It hurried one along, confused one with a barrage of impressions. In the world of creation, he had time to isolate the most significant impressions life had offered him and to find the meanings that were immanent in them. The process of creating a work of art was very much a voyage of discovery because it allowed time for him to be fully aware of the nature of his feelings as well as for clear intellectual analysis.

It was James's opinion that, properly treated, there was no area of experience which could not be made to yield artistic fruit. For his own part, he needed only to feel that a certain impression was important. He would then store it in his memory to be brooded over from time to time until the nature of what interested him in the impression became apparent. He accumulated his material on all sides, at social gatherings, while travelling on a train or strolling through a city, under the most common or under unusual conditions. Sometimes it was an overheard remark that served him for inspiration; a woman holding a certain pose could suffice. He sensed the drama implicit in the observation, and he had but to wait for its revelations. The raw material of life gathered in America, Europe, on board ship, in houses great and small, was placed in "the heavy bag of remembrance—of suggestion—of imagination—of art." All was brought eventually to Lamb House, Rye, to be taken out under a "mild still light . . . to take form like the gold and jewels of a mine."

When a writer in the naturalist tradition received an impression, his procedure was to explore all the details connected with his impression and try to reproduce in his work a situation identical with the one he had observed. James operated very differently. Once he received an impression he preferred not to learn of its ramifications in actuality. He liked best to let his *données* develop without any interference such as a knowledge of how the actual situation had been resolved might bring to bear. The thought of dragging in outside authority to support by reason and example an action of his stories would have seemed to James absurd. He had to be free to feel where the interest lay in his impression and free to develop it according to his own sense of things. In this respect, he seems to have had the quality which Keats observed Shakespeare to have possessed so enormously, *"Negative capability,* that is, when a man is capable of being in uncertainties, mysteries, doubts, without any irritable reaching after fact and reason."

Certain chance impressions might disclose a truth to the mind when years of intellectual effort would have kept it in ignorance. So profoundly conscious was James of this phenomenon that he caused the action of many of his finest works to turn on a person's sudden visual impression. There is Strether's shattering insight, in *The Ambassadors,* while he is gazing upon the river and a boat with two lovers, or, in *The Golden Bowl,* Maggie Verver's view through the window of another pair of lovers, or, in *The Portrait of a Lady,* Isabel Archer's glimpse of Osmond sitting and Madame Merle standing in the same room. These impressions, like the ones for which James himself was the "offered plate," require no logical or abstracting activity. What is offered to the view is present with all its implications to be felt and absorbed as a whole.

The ability to arrive at understanding through such penetrating flashes of intuition is by no means common property, and James illustrates in many short stories the blindness and futility of those who live by intellect alone. Sir Arthur Demesne, in *The Siege of London* (1883), is described as "... the victim of perplexities from which a single spark of direct perception would have saved him. He took everything in the literal sense; he had not a grain of humor." Sir Arthur was typical, to James's mind, of many individuals who rarely perceive the meaning of what happens to them. They are seldom aware of a unit of experience *as* a unit, with a grasp of how it developed, what elements affected its course, how various participants were involved in it, and how it was resolved. Often, they are so caught up in life, in the action itself, that they have no time to absorb all that an experience has to offer. Some individuals are so loosely organized emotionally and intellectually, that life can only affect them to produce a reflex action. Others are so encased by hard, anaesthetic layers of habit, propriety, custom, stereotyped thought, that little possibility exists of a felt perception between them and the events that comprise their lives.

The pathetic destiny of individuals who for one reason or another do not permit themselves to enter into any felt relationship with experience often claimed James's attention as a theme for fiction. The most notable instance is Lambert Strether of *The Ambassadors,* whose belated awakening to the aesthetic potentialities of life grew out of James's impression of William Dean Howells' life. It seemed to James that Howells was completely unequipped for anything like a broad appreciation of European life. Five years as a consul in Venice and subsequent tours in Europe had not broken through Howells' genteel fastidiousness. When Jonathan Sturges, a young writer, repeated to James the words of advice given to him by Howells, urging him "to live," James saw at once the nature of the tragedy involved. At bottom, it was the story of a man who had gained all the honors and rewards that usually go with a successful life but who realizes too late that in achieving these things he has sacrificed the greatest thing of all—life itself.

In a sense, it seemed to James that the British reading public was a victim of the same timidity, the same distrust of the senses, the same fear of a genuinely felt relationship. It was eager to join in vicarious adventures on far-off seas, or in stormy historical romances. With such vehicles it never really committed itself to an experience that demanded an active response to everything presented, that appealed to fine shades of feeling and thought, and required of each individual reader that he discover for himself the experience's meaning. In general, James found the British reading public did not want experience, but an escape from experience; it simply did not want to become involved.

There is no questioning the emotional intensity with which James approached literature; the evidence is overwhelming. His sensibilities seem always to have been keyed to a very high pitch. There was an incessant pressure to express, to resolve into a concrete artistic form at least some of his perceptions. James was completely dedicated to his task. Indeed, he suggests at times a priest, one vowed to serve in the tabernacle of art, seeing all of life as subject to the power of art and exercising his office with purity and beauty.

To make works of prose-fiction was a natural and a happy activity for him. Out of the continuous flow of sensation, the great flux of experience, certain perceived aspects appealed to him with peculiar intensity. These interacted with what he termed his "cultivated consciousness," that is, the great body of impressions upon which he had already expended thought and feeling. The original *donnée,* having undergone a synthesizing process in the "cultivated consciousness" much as a piece of meat might assimilate juices and flavors in a *pot-au-feu,* demanded to be served up as a work of art.

In the long and multicoloured shadow which fell between the *donnée* and the novel, James recognized feeling as the cohesive and impelling force. To deviate consciously from this felt power, to add or detract from the dictates of aesthetic feeling, was to run the risk of appearing "written," of appearing to be mechanically ordered. The story lost its life-giving principle and became, however lifelike, a marionette show. No amount of planning could substitute for the role of feeling in the creative process. No matter how much an author might plot and plan and calculate, what determined the nature of his work was the way he felt and saw and aesthetically conceived it. James did, of course, draw up sketches for stories and even elaborate scenarios in some instances. Still, the completed works show that he did not feel committed to following the preliminary plan—which was as often as not put together for the sake of an editor.

Once James commenced a story, he rarely knew where he was going to end up. The more he explored his material, the more he discovered that required expression. No matter how humble a theme he might select, once he commenced treating it the theme grew larger and larger, like the legendary beanstalk. Even when he succeeded in confining it within a certain space, it remained bursting with potentialities for growth. The more he traced out the implications of things, the more he came out upon fresh perspectives that required exploration. Usually James marked out these transitions from one set of explorations to another by shifting the scene and at least partially rearranging the set of characters selected as explorers.

Aesthetic sensitivity, the ability to respond imaginatively to suggestions of color and sound, to the spatial composition of

scenes, and other appearances is required of a reader by James.
He perceived his material aesthetically and presented it in such
a way that the reader might have similar perceptions. In his
mature work he is almost never seen, in the manner of Thack-
eray or Trollope, visibly directing the proceedings, or, like
George Eliot, interspersing his narrative with philosophical
observations. The reader must *feel* how the theme is being
treated; the reader who can follow James's pages only with his
intellect will miss their full effect. No one knew better than
James that relatively few readers were equipped, or for that
matter inclined, to partake of this aesthetic experience.

As James's technical ability developed he tried more and more
to create the kind of work that would involve the emotional as
well as intellectual responses of the reader. The novels become
more tightly unified, explore their themes with increasing caution; eventually each detail becomes related to the whole, contributing its bit to the total experience. In James's mature work
the reader is not "told," things are not explained for him, so
that he may grasp with his intellect alone what has happened.
As in actual life, he must depend upon his own moral sense,
must judge characters and actions as they appeal to him alone,
proceed through decisions and revisions, assurance and uncer-
tainty as the story unfolds. There is this major difference from
life: everything irrelevant to the unit of experience has been
excluded. This should help the reader, but he is thrown upon
his own resources and to a great extent the value of the experience will depend upon what he, himself, can bring to it.

It was James's opinion that the difference in the relationship
between the reader and a novel, and that existing between the
author and the actual experience from which the novel derived,
is a difference of degree rather than kind. When his brother
William objected to the ending of *The Europeans,* Henry wrote

to assure him that other story-tellers would have retained it. To the anticipated rejoinder that other readers would have wished it away, he countered, "But that is the same; for the teller is but a more developed reader."

As a reader, James would have satisfied the fondest hopes of an author who desired close, critical attention as well as "felt" response. All of James's discussion of books and authors testifies to the searching scrutiny he brought to bear upon what he read. His own search for technique made him sharply aware of problems connected with writing; and he analysed the novels that came his way with a regard to how he, in the author's place, would have handled the subject matter. This practice became habitual with him, and long after his unique style was clearly defined, he still subjected the work of other novelists to this process of reconstruction. He did his best to appreciate whatever was characteristic of a particular author's treatment, then set about applying his own. Sometimes this took place simultaneously. At times, he felt that his desire to rewrite what he was reading seriously interfered with his ability as a reader. The novel he could *only* read, he once remarked, he could not read at all. Such stories as *The Last of the Valerii,* suggested by Merimée's *La Vénus d'Ille,* and *Paste,* which gives another slant to Maupassant's famous *La Parure* (or possibly to an earlier version of that story), attest that James did not always confine to himself the desire to express his version of another writer's work.

One of the chief functions of the center, or centers, of consciousness in a James novel is to facilitate the reader's felt response. James considered it very important for this reason that the characters should acutely feel their situations. The reader would be most apt to benefit from a felt relationship if he were sharing the consciousness of someone who was "finely aware and richly responsible." James was so zealous in the matter of making his central figures get everything possible out of their experience, that he was at times hard pressed to reconcile their quality of mind with their station in life. This is the problem which confronted him in dealing with Hyacinth Robinson of *The Princess Casamassima.* James did not quite know how to make the poor, uneducated son of a seamstress acutely aware of his situation without making him unnatural. King Lear and Hamlet, because of the terrible acuity with which they perceived the heart of experience, were for James the ideal figures for a center of consciousness. With a hero of this kidney, the author could prepare for his reader a range of sensibility, a degree of intensity, that no amount of artistic solicitation could effect with such a one as Hyacinth Robinson.

James considered that at all costs the reader had to believe in the center of consciousness. If the reader trusted this character, his intellect would overlook even serious flaws in the story itself. This posed a special problem in such stories as *What Maisie Knew* and *The Pupil,* where James called upon children to demonstrate a sensitive perception of complex human situations. The children may not have an intellectual grasp of what is happening (although the intelligence they exhibit is sometimes astonishing), but they have a deep emotional response and can trust to their feelings to guide them through the maze. There are often many characters in James's novels more intelligent than the one through whose consciousness the reader experiences the story, but it is the chosen character's fine awareness and responsiveness that usually determine his central position. The unity and focus achieved through the use of a center of consciousness were artistic enhancements of great importance, and their value lay in that they supplied a closer felt relation with the experience than it was otherwise possible to achieve.

Sharing the consciousness of such a character as Newman in *The American* was, in James's opinion, "the act of personal possession of one being by another at its completest. . . ."

Again and again, both in his fiction and criticism, James stressed the relationship between feeling and time. Man needed time to feel, to know what his feelings were about; he needed time to cultivate shades and intensities of feeling; the artist, above all, needed time to cultivate his feelings. An individual life seemed to amount to very little in vast, impersonal London. It appeared to James that a man almost passed out of memory when it was his misfortune to die in that city. He deplored this impersonality, "the awful doom of general dishumanisation," and attributed it to the fact that people failed to take the necessary time to recognize their feelings about one another. People scurried about their affairs hardly pausing to register the disappearance of someone in their midst. "It takes space to feel, it takes time to know, and great organisms as well as small have to pause, more or less, to possess themselves and to be aware," James wrote in his Preface to *The Altar of the Dead*, a story based on such an attempt to pause and become aware. It was essential to recover through memory, not intellectual items, but things felt. Visions of the past, precious associations, valued moments, all came back through feeling, and this required self-possession and time.

James was fond of many modern developments. He took an almost childish delight in motoring. Yet he regretted the stepped-up pace that occurred during his lifetime. In the matter of travel alone, it seemed to him that the various means of swift transportation, the exhaustive travel literature on every country, the multiplying hordes of tourists forever in transit, had all made for an irrecoverable loss of experience. His biography of William Wetmore Story speaks of the generation that travelled by crude street-cars and even ox-carts, that lost touch with the world of affairs but had the necessary margin, "the time to make its discoveries and to know what it felt."

Place, as well as time, played a part in the effort to possess one's self and be aware. James found a certain amount of seclusion necessary in order to get the most out of his impressions. In Italy he found himself subject to so many and to such intense impressions that he could not properly assimilate them. Even London, which he adored despite any criticism he might make of it, came to have too many distractions and interruptions for him. He achieved his final and ideal situation in the autumn of 1897, when he leased Lamb House, Rye. It was far enough from London to discourage casual visitors and afforded an excuse to decline dinner invitations. A roomy, brick house atop the hill on which the town is built, it offered quiet, a sense of peace, and in its small garden house (destroyed by the one bomb to land on Rye during World War II) the work of art could progress with the leisure of an earlier age.

James could go back through the years in this timeless atmosphere and select the impressions that had been sufficiently mellowed for use. If original images had grown dim, so much the better for reflection, James thought, for then reflection would not be agitated by the original image, but would be both sharp and quiet. Time did not diminish the role played by feeling in this contemplative period, but greatly increased it by permitting the exploration of various possibilities. Out of the unformed mass of suggestion and impulse, the artist would eventually grasp "the tail of an idea" and proceed to the stage of expression.

As early as 1872 James indicated his belief that a period of detachment should intervene for the artist between an impression and its use in a work of art. James found fault with Taine for not having allowed for this kind of adjustment. He wrote of that critic's *English Literature*, "... in the nature of the case his treatment of the subject lacks that indefinable quality of spiritual initiation which is the tardy consummate fruit of a wasteful, purposeless, passionate sympathy."

The adjectives "purposeless" and "wasteful" ably characterize that period of crude groping, when possibilities are successively seized and abandoned, before the artist or critic finally sees the solution to his problem. The word "passionate" describes the persistent felt relation through which a sense of original impressions is retained. The word which James usually employed to describe this process is "reflection," and it is to be noted that he intended the term to refer by no means to an exclusively intellectual process, but rather to a process largely concerned with feeling.

It was to this process that James referred in 1893, when he wrote in one of his notebooks, "It all comes back to the old, old lesson—that of the art of *reflection*. When I practice it the whole field is lighted up—feel again the multitudinous presence of all human situation and pictures, the surge and pressure of *life*. All passions, all combinations are there."

Much could be expected of an impression dropped into such a *pot-au-feu* of experience. This treatment prevented the glib, automatic production of superficial work twisted to fit a predetermined form or simply spewed forth as unassimilated impressions. With time the artist could bring his funded experience to bear on an impression. Even in the most excited moments of actual creative activity, he would not betray the possibilities of his subject or of his craft. The fusion of deep feeling with clear, precise thinking which great artistry required was the substance of a discovery made by Peter Sherringham in *The Tragic Muse,* while he watched the performance of a great actress. James had this man meditate upon "... the perfect presence of mind, unconfused, unhurried by emotion, that any artistic performance requires and that all, whatever the instrument, require in exactly the same degree: the application, in other words, clear and calculated, crystal-firm, as it were, of the idea conceived in the glow of experience, of suffering, of joy."

The vital importance of allowing time for reflection to do its work is repeatedly emphasized by James in his last collection of critical studies, *Notes on Novelists.* James regrets that Balzac had allowed so little time for reflection. The value of Gilbert Cannan's work, James decided, might have quadrupled if he had been patient and allowed time for his impressions to develop. Possibly the finest illustration of James's belief on this matter occurs in a letter which he wrote to H. G. Wells in 1911.

Wells was one of many contemporary writers whose work James admired, but he recognized a fundamental cleavage between his own and Wells's way of regarding art. James considered that his way involved a great many problems over which Wells rode "roughshod and triumphant." It seemed to James that Wells's use of the autobiographic form begged the question of art; it became an excuse for simply jotting down whatever came first to hand and leaving it at that. James expressed his objection to Wells's method, in part, as follows: "There is, to my vision, no authentic, and no really interesting and no *beautiful,* report of things on the novelist's, the painter's part unless a particular detachment has operated, unless the great stewpot or crucible of the imagination, of the observant and recording and interpreting mind in short, has intervened and played its part—and this detachment, this chemical transmutation for the aesthetic, the representational, end is terribly wanting in autobiography brought, as the horrible phrase is, up to date." In using the phrase "the painter's part," James might have had in mind specifically his criticisms in *Picture and Text*

(1893) of the facile impressions rendered by John Singer Sargent.

James's discussions of his own writing offer abundant examples of how impressions have simmered in his mind for years before being put to use. It is possible to trace some of the strange changes these impressions have undergone and observe the unexpected combinations and transmutations, as well as their amazing persistence in his memory. There is, for example, the genesis of *The Spoils of Poynton*. On one occasion James perceived a *donnée* in a story told him of a threatened lawsuit between mother and son as a result of the son's effort to evict the mother from a dower-house to make room for his bride. On another occasion, a *donnée* came to him while visiting a place called Fox Warren. "I thought of the strange, the terrible experience of a nature with a love and passion for beauty, united by adverse circumstances to such a family and domiciled in such a house." One case involved a human relationship of extreme ugliness, the other an equally repulsive physical setting. James isolated these two *données* from their context in actuality to gain the largest amount of freedom for treatment.

Eventually the two became fused. Through reflection and the alchemy of the creative process, they emerged in a work of art that placed its emphasis upon a noble nature interacting with a background of the rarest beauty. All of the grim bitterness that characterized the conditions of the original inspirations finds expression in the story, but James has thrown into relief the other side of the coin. The human failings are put into their proper perspective through James's emphasis upon a sharply realized vision of human conduct that is morally beautiful. Fox Warren has become the exquisite Poynton. James successfully projected "the possible other case"; the role of feeling had played its part.

5

*. . . I seemed to feel it in me to respond a little—
to see it as an idea with which something might be
done. But voyons un peu what it might possibly
amount to. The thing is not worth doing at all unless something tolerably big and strong is got out
of it. But the only way that's at all luminous to
look at it is to see what there may be in it of most
eloquent, most illustrative and most human—most
characteristic and essential: what is its real, inner-
most, dramatic, tragic, comic, pathetic, ironic note.
The primary interest is not in any mere grotesque
picture of follies and misadventures, of successes
and sufferings: it's in the experience of some creature that sees it and knows and judges and feels it
all, that has a part to play in the episode, that is
tried and tested and harrowed and exhibited by it
and that forms the glass, as it were, through which
we look at the diorama. James,* Notebooks *(November 8, 1894).*

Dramatic Substance

THE STARTING POINT FOR JAMES'S FICTION WAS USUALLY SOME
impression which struck him so forcefully as being the nucleus
of a work of art that it seemed a gift from life. These impressions he called *données*. Other writers received these gifts too,
and they promptly incorporated them in their work even as
they might make prompt use of a gift lamp to light their study
or convert a gift pumpkin into a pie. James regarded his gifts
differently. He received them as the hero of a fairy tale might
receive his gifts, in awe of their possibilities, discovering in the
lamp the presence of a genie and in the pumpkin the glittering
beauty of a coach and six.

James learned never to accept a *donnée* at its face value as
merely an isolated bit of experience. The scene witnessed, the
remark overheard, whatever it was that constituted one of these

données, had its value in that it brought into sudden focus a general stream of thought and feeling. In order to perceive precisely what material constituted the *donnée,* James had to feel it out cautiously and over an extended period of time. Only in this way would he lay bare the tensions, oppositions and relations implicit in its structure. He sensed that there was drama in his bit of substance, and he had to allow the drama to unfold.

James speaks in the Preface to *What Maisie Knew* of how he would inspect a *donnée* with his "intellectual nostril," to discover its quality and what kind of fruit it might eventually yield. Using another metaphor, he describes how he would feel himself "in presence of the red dramatic spark that glowed at the core of my vision and that, as I gently blew upon it, burned higher and clearer." The sensuous terms James employs in these metaphors suggest the aesthetic nature of his treatment of the *donnée,* for whatever dramatic elements might be enclosed there had to be perceived by the senses.

William James had advanced the startling proposition that just as colors, odors, and sounds registered upon the senses, so relationships such as those described by prepositions—"with," "from"—could be immediately experienced. The same held true, he maintained, of the most complex ideas; they arouse a definite sentiment and are actually "experienced." This discovery has been considered by some to be his greatest contribution to psychology and forms the basis of his radical empiricism. As early as 1884, Henry James was dealing with this same idea. Whether or not it was William's investigations that gave Henry insight into aesthetic processes, the latter's observation illustrates in regard to the artist what the former discovered to be true for people in general.

If, then, the expansion of the *donnée* into a novel involved a great deal of intellectual activity, the intellect was chiefly concerned with probing the conflicts and affinities felt to exist in material that was conceived in aesthetic terms. The imagination had definite scenes and characters, as well as concrete situations, with which to work. Similarly, the past experience summoned to bear upon the *donnée* was so selected and controlled as to operate for specific purposes—to supply examples, sensuous details—so that reminiscence was not vague or loosely emotional, but to the aesthetic point. It would be misleading to speak of James's "method" in developing a *donnée* to the stage where it was ready for expression in literary form. The development was so much a matter of inquiring, experimenting, and trusting to feeling for a sense of what was the right way, that it could be more aptly described as a negation of method.

The artist's felt response to his material was considered by James to constitute the essence of his awareness of its real and potential drama. For this reason James insisted on protecting the integrity of that felt response. He wished to isolate his impression from its context in actuality, to stow it away in his mind and with time establish his personal sense of what was significant in the impression that made it "his germ, his vital particle, his grain of gold." If a friend was telling James an anecdote in which the latter recognized a *donnée,* he would try not to hear any amplification of the anecdote. By establishing his own relation to the subject, ferreting out just where its interest lay for him, James could nourish it from his experience and cultivate the potentiality he sensed in it. His desire to imagine for himself the course of the drama he sensed in the impression sprang partly from the knowledge that life usually bungled such matters, that the fine possibilities in a situation hardly ever were the ones that materialized. But it sprang even more from the knowledge that the artist's all-important personal, felt response had no opportunity to establish itself if he were in too direct association with his impression. Under such a condition the artist became little more than a machine reproducing images of actuality.

James depicted in *The Real Thing* the necessity of the artist to choose a subject which afforded latitude for imaginative treatment. To allow the original image to grow dim, to use it as a kind of source from which a constant and thickening stream of reflection initiated was a way to achieve this latitude. *The Real Thing* concerns an artist who was to execute a series of sketches of fashionable English people. An elderly couple, Major and Mrs. Monarch, perfect examples of the type he wished to portray, were in desperate need of money and offered themselves to him as models. He hired them on the spot, but after several efforts realized that he could not work from them. They had the faces, figures, manner, clothes, every gesture and line; nevertheless, he discovered that to stick to these models was to produce artistic trash. He found himself constrained to a mechanical reproduction of actuality. There was no room for the operation of imagination, of the artist's personal sense of things and no opportunity for a penetration of the pose to what he felt was basically true of the type. Major and Mrs. Monarch, perfect to the last detail, forbade the alteration of any particularity. The substance of art never came alive in the artist's mind as a thing of tensions, climaxes, resolutions, inciting comparisons from memory, swelling into unexpected possibilities; it remained an image to be transferred from the retina of the eye to the canvas.

James's concept of the substance of art as a drama of felt relations unfolding within the consciousness of the artist was completely at variance with the dominant trend of his time. Naturalism, which was to carry not only the day but the succeeding half-century, boasted that it dispensed with the artist's personal feelings. It was scientific, objective, dispassionate. The most important French writers were at pains to reflect this theory in their work. The English novelists, too, leaped somewhat clumsily on the bandwagon, and brought with them an enormous baggage of details. Such "new" novelists as Arnold Bennett and H. G. Wells crammed their works with observations until they were ready to burst at the seams, but just what interest was supposed to attach to these vast collections, James often protested to be at a loss to know.

A favorite dogma of the new writers was that they were presenting "a slice of life." This was, to James's mind, a meaningless phrase since there was no question of a slice upon which the further question of how you slice it did not hang. Choice and comparison, someone's personal decision, had to operate at some point. Writers of Zola's school had not only made a deliberate selection of material, in James's opinion, but they had chosen to present the worst aspects of human nature. They were guilty of clinging obstinately and perversely to this choice in spite of any finer aspects of human nature that might be revealed to them. They did not permit their impressions to develop dramatic oppositions, to establish relations with the whole of life and especially with life's nobler portions. The consequence was that the substance from which they put together their novels was not a personally felt human drama, but a set of tableaux held as community property and depicting the seven deadly sins.

Even in cases where the artist did have a strong personal feeling for his subject matter, James considered him at fault if he did not express those dramatic elements in which he felt the interest to center. James was unalterably opposed to the all-inclusive mixture, the life *en masse,* in the work of Tolstoy and Dostoevsky. Both of these writers, he recognized, had an enormously broad and intensely felt body of experience. Their writings attested to this and to their genius. Nevertheless, because of a lack of composition, much of this experience tended to dissipate and go to waste. James would have found support for this charge from Tolstoy himself, who, in his discussion of aesthetics, stood out for the necessity of form in order to communicate feeling exactly to the receptor. He found the complexity of his own works objectionable; it compromised clarity, sincerity, and the "infectiousness" of feeling. Looseness of form, James considered, caused the dramatic substance of Tolstoy's and Dostoevsky's work to relax into a "fluid pudding." It retained a remarkable quality only because those writers had responded to life with a burning intensity of feeling. By contrast, the great artistry, the rigorous selection involved in Flaubert's expression failed to give force and beauty to his subject because something prevented him from developing the drama he felt in life.

The practice by which critics, editors, and the public determined what was suitable subject matter for art was another major factor in short-circuiting the artist's felt relationship with his material. Because of certain popular moral patterns, or such conventions as the happy ending, many novelists found the treatment of their material determined for them in advance. An excessive concern with technical effects could also lead an artist to sacrifice his felt perceptions, and in this respect James found himself hoist with his own petard. In his early works, he recognized, the manner was often more apparent than the matter, and even quite late in his career he would sometimes experiment with technique at the expense of his subject. Nevertheless, the more he studied the art of fiction, the more he was convinced that he would be most successful as an artist by cleaving to his felt perceptions and letting these determine the treatment.

James's conviction that "The distinguished thing is the firm hand that weaves the web, the deep and ingenious use made of the material . . ." led him to insist not only that artists should be free to treat whatever aspects of experience appealed to them, but that no artist had a right to claim any particular subject as his exclusive property. Since the treatment, based on the artist's personal feeling, was the important thing, it was illogical to think of a subject as belonging to any one author. James wholeheartedly agreed that "the style is the man," and argued that possession attached solely to the way in which an artist treated his material. For this reason it is superficial to talk of someone writing "like" someone else, or using someone else's subject. The fact that a work of art is the fruit of an individual artist's identity is enough to guarantee its being different enough.

For this same reason James considered an author free to treat the same subject as often as he wished. In his own writing he returned again and again to a comparison of American and European values. He treated it from both American and European points of view, its manifestation in art, marriage, society and in other ways. If an artist truly examined his personal sense of a given subject and tried to express what he felt, it seemed to James that his work would have originality. Furthermore, each time he returned to a given subject he would discover fresh combinations and emphases amongst its elements, especially since, with time, he would himself have altered. About the only rule that James thought should apply to the author's treatment of his subject was the one, artistically imposed, whereby he should seek to express the aspect of his subject that most interested him. In this regard, James pictured the artist as "a nimble besieger or nocturnal sneaking adventurer, who perpetually plans, watches, circles for penetrable places"; he must

find his own way through the great blank walls of the commonplace to discover and lead forth the object most precious to him.

James found it essential that such an approach be made in
terms of specific human situations. The command "Dramatise,
dramatise!" which he wrote in his notebook upon discovering
a *donnée*, suggests his urgent effort to cultivate his dramatic
substance in aesthetically perceptible terms. He had to see his
characters, listen to their voices, and grow aware of the background which set off their personalities. The *donnée* almost
always had meanings of the most general nature, but James did
not think in abstract terms, as has been noted. He once remarked about Turgenieff: ". . . an idea, with him, is such and
such an individual, with such a hat and waistcoat, bearing the
same relation to it as the look of a printed word does to its
meaning." This became true of James at a very early stage in
his career. He received all his impressions in dramatic form
and even seemed unable to conceive of anything independent
of it. There was hardly such a thing as an unembodied idea for
him.

If Turgenieff did not conceive his ideas in the abstract, there
still could be no doubt that his stories had a meaning that spread
far beyond the given situation, and that powerful ideas could
easily be abstracted from his stories. The various sketches in
Memoirs of a Sportsman offer a dramatic picture of social in-
justice and human character. The themes that flow through the
work were appearing at the time it was composed as reasoned,
abstract manifestoes from the pens of other writers. His *données*
were dramatically interesting because they had connections
with and into life. They were not what James called "cases."
A case might be curious and even fascinating, but it was essentially arbitrary and isolated, a collection of circumstances that
offered nothing for reflection, and represented nothing that

could be more generally applied to life. James once described such a case as possessing "no moral or morality," nor having any "projected out of it as an interest. Hence the so *unfertilised* state in which the mutual relations are left! Thereby it's only theatrically, as distinguished from dramatically, interesting."

It is important to note in this connection that what fertilizes subject matter and thereby makes growth possible is the artist's sense of dramatic oppositions within the subject matter. If the growth of these oppositions takes on a moral quality, it will be because the moral sense of the artist has been at work upon them. Somewhere in his *données* James was conscious of a struggle, and as he delved into the heart of his material the center of interest emerged as a moral struggle. This was so because what chiefly interested James about experience was the struggle between good and evil. He proceeded in his fiction to express his sense of this struggle as it manifested itself in experience, bringing suspense, curiosity and anxiety into play, building up tensions and posing the final question of victory or failure. It was no good to intersperse an action with moral reflections, James felt, nor was it of any use to unbalance the familiar conditions of life in such a way that virtue and evil are always apparent as such and the issue of their struggle never in doubt. James was not preparing a catechism for his readers; he was providing them with the material for a moral experience. The reader has to become aware through his own sense of the struggle and tensions of what is morally involved.

Just what, by way of the dramatic, a situation might offer, could only be determined through the actual process of expression. The first step in this direction was to provide the reader with some difficulty, with presented figures and a constituted scene, to make him aware of personalities and of the dynamic interaction of forces. Until this condition had been met, James held that writing remained within the realm of extravagant verbiage.

It is possible to see in James's notebooks the vigilance he maintained over his work to insure a treatment that did illustrate something. He scrapped his first beginning for *The Real Thing* because it did not seem to grow organically out of the *donnée*. He reminded himself that "One must put a little action —not a stupid, mechanical arbitrary action, but something that is of the real essence of the subject . . ." into the work. The successive climaxes of a James novel usually spring from a revelation of character. The central figures are not static personalities, set types responding automatically to traditional stimuli. The action of the novel is morally crucial to the individuals involved. As they undergo it and perceive its meaning, their conduct becomes indicative of their individual natures and of their spiritual depth. James discovered more and more about his characters as he dealt with them, and there is a corresponding gradual process of discovery for the reader. A character's physical description and relevant background are usually given to the reader early. Understanding of that character, however, comes only as his personality gradually unfolds through the action of the story. It is provided in slow stages so that the reader gradually becomes aware and proceeds to deeper levels of understanding.

One of the principal attractions Turgenieff's method of writing had for James was the way he placed characters together and let the story unfold from their interaction with one another. As early as 1866, James had expressed his belief that the novel, as an art form, seemed far worthier when it was in this way concerned with an understanding of human nature, than when its purpose was "the entertainment of those jolly barbarians of taste who read novels only for what they call the 'story.' " Like Turgenieff, James was to find his work most successful when he proceeded by "investing some conceived or encountered individual, some brace or group of individuals, with the germinal property and authority."

This was to become the basic pattern of his *données,* the essence of their dramatic quality. His novels, particularly those of the major phase, are dramas of the consciousness because the interest lies in the minds of the characters. The reader is privileged to experience their reactions to impressions, to feel their sensitive adjustment, their analysis of what is happening to them; he shares their confusions and assists in formulating tentative hypotheses for action. But as he progresses, the critical reader is aware of James's consciousness shaping events, of James's moral sense pervading the work and shaping it with a kind of inevitability towards some culmination that is morally beautiful.

The "roundness" of James's characters comes in part from his impressions of their archetypes in real life, but more so from the thoroughness with which he conceived them in his imagination. Similarly, the dramas in which he imagined them to be engaged were thoroughly felt by James because he took the time to feel all the implications of these dramas, to compare them with similar dramas he had known in actuality, and to express them with elaborate concentration. At times, such characteristics as the precocity of James's children, the capacity of his heroines for renunciation, the general subtlety of his characters, seem overdrawn. Yet, there is no sense of their discontinuity with the rest of humanity. Through being so sensitive and aware, so capable of renunciation, sympathy, and kindness, the figures in James's dramatic substance belong to a small piece of humanity, but it is a piece that is richly representative of the whole.

6

*A novel is a living thing, all one and continuous,
like any other organism, and in proportion as it
lives will it be found, I think, that in each of the
parts there is something of each of the other parts.*
James, The Art of Fiction *(1884).*

Organic Form

AS HENRY JAMES SET ABOUT EXPRESSING THE DRAMATIC SUBSTANCE
of his *données,* he found that his material tended almost inevitably to group itself in terms of successive scenes. As his
style evolved, he found himself building always toward certain
key scenes; for crucial developments dramatic writing came
more and more to replace narrative, until such narrative writing as he did use was employed as preparation for culminating
dramatic scenes. James's practice of conceiving his developments in terms of scenes, while it was always essential to his
aesthetic grasp of his material, came to play a central part in
the structure of his novels and in effecting their organic unity.

The idea of "scenes" as concentrated emotional moments
had been with James from the first. He relates an incident in
A Small Boy and Others from the summer of 1854 that first
suggested to him the idea of scenes. He was visiting some cousins,
and when it came time for the young daughter, Marie, to go
to bed, she uttered the immemorial objections: ". . . a protest
and an appeal in short which drew from my aunt the simple
phrase that was from that moment so preposterously to 'count'
for me. 'Come now, my dear; don't make a scene—I *insist* on
your not making a scene!' That was all the witchcraft the occasion used, but the note was none the less epoch-making." "Life
at these intensities," James noted, "clearly became 'scenes.' " It

89

was as though all the participants somehow agreed tacitly to embark upon a unit of experience set off by an intensity of feeling from what might proceed or follow it. Such was James's early impression. Before many years had passed, he was a constant observer of scenes, not simply of the haphazard kind offered by life, but of those offered by art. A little more than two decades after his experience with Marie, he was an inveterate theater-goer at the Comédie Francaise at a time when Sarah Bernhardt was an ingenue.

A prolonged exposure to the art of the theater had far-reaching effects upon James. Until he was over fifty, he was convinced that his real gifts were those of a playwright and his greatest ambition was to write successful plays. It was not until the mid-1890's that he finally abandoned hope of achieving success in that profession. All the while he had been writing short-stories and novels, adapting the skills he learned from the theater to these literary forms. The thematic substance of his novels came to be expressed through successive scenes, one evolving organically out of another in a manner comparable to the successive stages of development in a plant. The work drew its sustenance from the artist's experience, and though each stage brought its revelations, its full meaning could be comprehended only when it achieved its final growth.

Intimately connected with his development of the scenic method of story-telling is James's use of the center of consciousness as a unifying device, one calculated to insure the closest relationship between the viewer and the thing viewed. In James's account of little Marie's effort to put off going to bed, the center of interest does not lie in whether or not her efforts were successful. The interest lies in the mind of the little boy who witnessed the action and in his examination of his reactions to it. The reader shares the discoveries of the little boy in his efforts to comprehend his impression. Even James's account of his discovery of scenes takes the form of a scene, and the reader is aided in his discoveries by means of a center of consciousness.

James's account of his childhood, particularly of his responsiveness to impressions, suggests his use of the child Maisie as a center of consciousness in *What Maisie Knew* (1897). She, too, had acquired the habit of silently watching, of listening intently, and of piecing together meanings from her fragmentary knowledge of the complex adult world in which she found herself. Her whole participation in life seemed to be restricted to what she could wrest from such spectatorship. Like James, she seemed to be a spectator witnessing her own history.

But Maisie's inaction at the center of a whirlwind of marriages, divorces, quarrels and love-making is apparent rather than real. Her own hopes and fears are woven into the context, and her efforts to cope with her experience form a large part of the novel's substance. Just as the scene is form or substance depending upon one's critical approach, so the center of consciousness can be said to fit both categories. Maisie's unusual viewpoint, naive and incomplete, always places the noblest construction upon behavior and contrasts with the outlook of her parents in a chiaroscuro of the morally beautiful and the morally ugly. Far from being a mere shuttlecock in the hard-fought game played by her elders, Maisie unifies the action and gives it a point of reference. Her vision of the successive scenes that comprise the action is the essential controlling factor in the organic development of the novel.

But James's handling of scenes in *What Maisie Knew* represents a late stage in the evolution of his method. He was attracted to the use of scenes during the 'seventies noting the careful attention given to the appearance of things by the French writers who practiced it most successfully. The reader had a continuous vision of places and people, and this made for a general continuity of his felt relationship with the work of art. Most of the novels James admired, however, presented a kaleidoscope of sensuous images; while this strengthened the reader's aesthetic response, the total effect was apt to be somewhat diffuse. James cut down sharply on the number of scenes to be presented to the reader, restricted them to scenes viewed by one or at most a very few centers of consciousness, and made each scene a careful impression that compressed and confined a great burden of meaning into its sensuous details. The result of this was that as James's technique matured the scenic method came to mean purity and economy of treatment as well as a sharply realized pattern of images. All of this both simplified and concentrated the job of the reader; he had relatively few scenes to deal with, but aesthetically they were so intimately related to the theme of the story that they demanded much closer scrutiny on his part. The character Allan Wayworth in James's story *Nona Vincent* is presented as a devotee of the scenic idea. He praises enthusiastically its purity, dignity, and architectural quality. It appeals to him especially because of its leanness and tightness, and he compares it to a ship from which all excess cargo must be jettisoned if it is to ride the waves.

James's use of the term "architectural" here in connection with the scenic method is of particular significance. Frequently he linked the terms "drama" and "architecture" when he sought to describe the form of a work as being at once simple, massive, and thoroughly unified. From the time when he first sent travel sketches back for publication in the newspapers and magazines at home, James had been a student of European architecture. His appreciation went beyond the usual surface admiration;

he was highly sensitive to such qualities as the disposition of masses, the arrangement of visible and invisible supports, the elements of thrust, tension, balance and counterbalance—to all of these he responded with feeling. Cathedrals, castles, elaborate villas, and formal country houses provided him with a constant source of inspiration because of the way in which they synthesized materials, colors, ornaments into a unified whole. They appealed to him also as a symbolic synthesis of a complex range of spiritual and social values.

It was with this awareness of the possibilities of architecture that James sometimes employed the term "architectural form" to those of his dramatic efforts that unfolded with great amplitude in space and time. The older James grew, the more he wanted to achieve architectural effects. Unfortunately, he could seldom permit himself this luxury; in order to get his work published he all too often had to choose subjects that required a minimum of dramatic treatment, or even no dramatic treatment at all. In the latter case, he employed an anecdotic form. When he was allowed space for some dramatic treatment, to cultivate at least some of the possibilities of his subject, his form became "the beautiful and blest nouvelle." When he was free to develop fully his subject, he thought in terms of architectural form. On such occasions he recorded in his notebooks his desire for "contact with the DRAMA, with the little difficult, artistic, ingenius, architectural FORM," and of his wish to do *"the* thing," ". . . the desire to get back only to the *big* (scenic, constructive 'architectural' effects) seizes me and carries me off my feet. . . . *Begin* it—and it will grow." At such moments James's shaping ideal emerges as monumental, yet classic in its purity and simplicity, and with a dynamic interaction of forces distributing life throughout its structure.

It seemed to James that if the exponents of naturalism made

an effort to exercise the economy required by the use of scenes, or if they had an awareness of architectural form, especially as it pertained to unity, proportion, and the subordination of the parts to the whole, a great deal could be salvaged from their heaps of unassimilated material. The facility of the naturalists in gathering facts surpassed the romance writers' gift of invention. But whether the novelist chose to write romance or to compile literal facts, he still had to make some effort to get a coherent total structure, or the result would be excessive waste. The same looseness which James found in so many of the followers of naturalism, he found in the work of romance writers such as George Sand. It seemed to him that her great ease of expression acted in many instances to her detriment, expanding into the unessential or meretricious. A predominant looseness would hinder any work from living long, he observed, and if it should live in spite of looseness, it was "only because closeness has somewhere, where it has most mattered, played a part."

It is important to bear in mind that James's ideas on the aesthetic nature of substance and form evolved over a considerable period of time, and while these ideas have direct implications for his later work, they only bear loosely upon the work written prior, say, to *The Portrait of a Lady* (1881). Similarly, it must be remembered that many of the English novelists James criticised for their lack of form, particularly in "The New Novel," were at an early stage in their careers and their grasp of technique was still uncertain. But time has brought added support to James's criticism of those novelists, both in America and in England, who were affected by naturalism.

On aesthetic grounds, he objected to the absence of an intrinsic relation of the various parts in their work; he found no sense of unity and wholeness, nor the feeling of organic growth. The massiveness of a work alone did not necessarily affect its artistic success adversely. It could, on the contrary, be a factor contributing to grandeur, as with certain Roman buildings. James found these structures huge, yet simple, with great lines, great spaces, parts boldly prominent and parts quietly reserved, yet it was not these elements alone that produced the air of a grand style. "It was all really, with the very swagger of simplicity, a wrought refinement, a matter of the mixture of the elements, a question, like everything else indeed in the whole place, of the mutual relation of parts."

Just as each part of a building had to enter into harmonious relation with the other parts, so each building in a group had to be suitably adapted if the group was to be aesthetically perceived as a whole. James noted this in connection with the view at Riverside Heights, and it led him to speculate upon "the entirely relative nature and value of 'treatment.' " A subject that would demand a specific kind of treatment if it were to stand as an art-object by itself would require another kind of treatment if it were to serve as part of an art-object. This illustrates, again, that the relation between form and substance is not a fixed one.

Once a character or incident that might serve for an anecdote is incorporated into the development of a novel, the kind and degree of emphasis extended it there, the selection or alteration to which it may be subject, is far different from the treatment in the smaller context. The character or incident assumes a contributory value in the novel, and serves as an element of the unified aesthetic experience. Conversely, each part of the aesthetic whole takes on a tone and has its meaning qualified through its interrelation with the other parts. This conception of form as organic has no tolerance for such familiar irrelevancies as moral or political digressions, characters and incidents introduced for "comic relief," or superfluous descriptive detail.

The most interesting question an artist has to consider, James said in the Preface to *Roderick Hudson,* is how to give the image and sense of certain things, while still keeping them subordinate to the whole and in relation to the other parts. This involved the necessity of summarizing and foreshortening, and yet keeping the essential values "both rich and sharp." During the composition of *Roderick Hudson,* James was aware of a running battle between his discursive imagination and his critical sense. Once an idea had satisfied the principle of continuity, there remained the problem of recognizing all of its relations to the development and treating those which directly affected it.

James wanted to use two themes in *The Tragic Muse.* One was his "political case," and the other his "theatrical case." The artistic problem he thereby confronted was that of sacrificing unity and keeping the two themes independent, or pursuing what would be the more difficult and aesthetically desirable policy of fusing the two. His discussion of this difficulty noted that many great artists, especially Tintoretto, had shown several actions taking place at once in the same picture without any apparent loss of authority. Novelists, too, had offered a variety of "pictures" in one novel. These works, however, like Tolstoy's *War and Peace,* he lumped together as "large, loose baggy monsters," since they exhibited so many violations of organic unity. His final decision was, of course, for fusion and he noted, "There is life and life, and as waste is only life sacrificed and thereby prevented from 'counting,' I delight in a deep-breathing economy and an organic form."

The unity achieved in *The Tragic Muse* is an aesthetic unity. The "political case" and the "theatrical case" are embodied in convincing personalities who are intimately involved with a central character. The contrasted ideals attract and repel, are subdued or highlighted through the interaction of these characters. There is an aesthetic quality binding together the variety of scenes. The reader can grasp how the central theme is being treated, and even when it expands into a complex pattern, he does not lose his awareness of a fundamental unity, of the relevance of each part to the whole.

Once an artist decided upon the course of treatment demanded by a certain view of a subject, James considered that he was obligated to follow it consistently. He could not deviate from it in order to include some choice scene that had but a tangential reference to the theme of the novel. Under certain conditions, James could have included a passage between Lady Davenant and young Wendover in *A London Life;* it was a scene he was sorely tempted to write, but according to the course he chose to follow, such a scene was impossible. This led him to remark: ". . . the beauty of a thing of this order really done as a whole is ever, certainly, that its parts are in abject dependence, and that even any great charm they might individually and capriciously put forth is infirm so far as it doesn't measurably contribute to a harmony." Parts have to be organically related to the whole, and there should be a just subordination of part to whole. The artist should determine where the center of interest lies and distribute emphasis accordingly. A common violation of this principle, James pointed out, was in the treatment of sex in French and Italian novels, where the emphasis upon sheer physical actions usurped all of the interest, leaving none for considerations of a more general significance.

On occasion James was sorely tempted to violate some of his own principles. When he was planning *The Sense of the Past,* he wanted to accentuate the role played by the portrait featured in that work. Such an emphasis did not seem to fit in with his general vision of the work. Still, he did not wish to abandon the idea and he reassured himself, ". . . nothing is an excrescence that I may interestingly, that I may contributively, work in." The most notable instances of James's working in material not strictly organic in its relation to the story occur in connection with his *ficelles.*

James termed certain characters in his major works *ficelles,* since like the twine binding a package, they were expected to help bind the story together. The problem he faced was to convert their artificial relation with the story into a real one. The *ficelles* often operate like the chorus of a drama, reviewing what has happened, commenting on its meaning and foreshadowing what is to come. Mr. and Mrs. Dexter Freer of *Lady Barberina* are representative of the type. They are not so colorful themselves as to compete with the main characters for the reader's interest; "they were grey rather, of monotonous hue." They, like other *ficelles,* are given to constant analysis of the characters and events that make up their lives and see to it that little should be lost for the reader. Their lives have been spent largely in a close scrutiny of events, and they have a deep well of shared experience from which they can draw up pieces for comparison and contrast with the present course of events. Thus, if the *ficelles* were a foreign element in the novel's organism, they were nevertheless one which promoted its growth.

But usually James was able to assimilate the *ficelles* as part of the essential drama of his work. Mrs. Assingham not only discourses with her husband on the action, but is more than literally instrumental in smashing the golden bowl. Henrietta Stackpole is magnified in *The Portrait of a Lady* to symbolize an aspect of American life. Maria Gostrey of *The Ambassadors* serves as a confidante and admirer of Strether, but she also helps round out the character of Madame de Vionnet. Each *ficelle* is a plea for discriminating attention to what is happening. While their organic relation to the story may be weak, they still belong "intimately to the treatment," to the dramatic structure of the novel.

According to James's theory, if a novel had a genuinely organic growth, it would be just as impossible to extract a character or scene from a completed work as it would be to include one having no intrinsic relation to it. Not only was it impossible to remove an individual element, but the "story," the "plot," could not be separated from the work and have much value as being representative of the work. This also held true for a section of dialogue or description. Once removed from their organic relation to the whole art object, these elements lose their distinctive character. They are the product of the carefully prepared development preceding their occurence and of an evolving interaction with the reader. Without the awareness which is a cumulative result of this prior experience, they cannot be properly perceived.

James thought that the only possible way in which the "plot" or "story" of a novel could be spoken of as a thing apart from the organic whole was as the *donnée*, the starting point. Even this, however, would correspond but faintly to the substance of the novel after it had been expressed by the artist. Indeed, to the extent that an idea *has* been expressed by the artist, it cannot be extracted from the art-object. James compared the relationship existing between the story and the novel, the idea and the form, to a needle and its thread and added, "I never heard of a guild of tailors who recommended the use of the thread without the needle, or the needle without the thread."

The work of art should be able to justify itself as an aesthetic whole, without need of any artificial supports, such as statistics, confirmatory reasoning, the citing of authorities and so forth to support its validity. The integrity of the work would be violated by such supports. Once the reader becomes involved with the complex of relations at work in a novel, he has to exercise a certain amount of faith as to their reality, and it is a proof of the artist's skill that this faith is not violated. The reader is expected to experience the work of art, and if in so doing he feels the impressions he is receiving—of things, characters, relationships—are false, he is privileged to reject the work as a failure.

To grasp for confirmation of the conditions of the novel from outside its context would be an artistic flaw, in James's opinion, and, in addition, a violation of the reader's offered faith. One of the reasons why he was fond of the ghost story was that it allowed an almost complete freedom to the imagination and at the same time positively relied upon a "conscious and cultivated credulity," on the part of the reader. It was as though the reader agreed to accept the ghosts so long as the experience to which they contributed was as genuine, as "realistic," as the experiences otherwise provided by life.

The endeavor to give full expression to an idea had almost always to make terms with the limitations of space. James tried to avoid the anecdotal form as much as possible as it allowed for the least development and organic treatment. He had to rewrite *The Middle Years* a number of times in order to reduce it to its final length. *Greville Fane* was "a minor miracle of foreshortening," and *The Abasement of the Northmores* and *The Tree of Knowledge* achieved the duplicity of masquerading as anecdotes although they were actually compressed novels. The brevity of these works was attained only by "innumerable repeated chemical reductions and condensations" that tended to make the short story one of the costliest forms of composition because of the amount of life that had to be sacrificed. James compared it with the sonnet form in the Preface to *The Author of Beltraffio* as "one of the most indestructible forms of composition in general use."

James preferred, even with short stories, to develop the dramatic oppositions latent in his *donnée* and produce a work that illustrated something about life as a whole. He wanted to exhibit delicate shadings, to see one thing through another and still another through that, to see all the dimensions of an idea and produce the effect of "truth diffused, distributed and, as it were atmospheric." When he succeeded in doing this, he termed the form a *nouvelle,* rather than a short story. It was a form he had grown familiar with through his study of Turgenieff, Balzac, and Maupassant. What it could lead to is witnessed by *The Pupil,* where the penetrating and many-shaded vision of Morgan Moreen and his tutor is brought to bear upon a group illustrative of the strange figures who frequented such cultural centers as Florence before the heavy Anglo-American invasions.

Whether James developed his subject generously or sparingly, the substance was always wedded to the form. Once the two had been joined by the sacrament of expression, it was impossible to separate them—provided the marriage was a true one. If it had not been a perfect fusion, there would be evidence of strain, of the artificial linkage, and critics would be free to play up the scandal of a possible breach. James would have been the first to welcome such scandal-mongering for he thought that, generally speaking, both critics and artists were too heedless of questions of form. When a critic did put forth a plea for form, he was apt to be "as blankly met as if his plea were for trigonometry." For his own part, James believed the form of a work of art was as much of the essence of that work as the idea. He believed it could be interesting in itself and yet so inseparable as never to exist merely for its own sake; it owed its life to being genuine and whole. James concluded that such a work as *Madame Bovary* was a classic ". . . because the thing, such as it is, is ideally *done,* and because it shows that in such doing eternal beauty may dwell."

7

The moving accident, the rare conjunction, whatever it be, doesn't make the story—in the sense that the story is our excitement, our amusement, our thrill and our suspense; the human emotion and the human attestation, the clustering human conditions we expect presented, only make it. James, Preface to The Altar of the Dead *(1904).*

The Drama of Consciousness

WHAT INTERESTED JAMES MOST ABOUT LIFE WAS SOMETHING HE would have called "the interest behind the interest." The spectacle of life had interest; the sheer sights and sounds of cities, of people going about the business of living, could compel his unflagging attention. James was a socially active person and had a huge circle of friends. Their personalities, adventures, and small-talk all had interest for him. Above all, however, he was interested in what went on in people's minds. He wanted to know how they felt about things, what their thoughts were, and the effort to find out by reflecting upon what clues came his way was an exciting kind of adventure for him. This search into "the interest behind the interest" made up the drama staged in the consciousness, and it became almost an artistic principle with James to present this drama for his readers with only the essential clues. When his career was in full stride, he had reached the point of permitting a gesture, a phrase, a chance observation to do the work on which other novelists would have lavished screams, wounds, and the divorce courts.

James trusted that what interested him would interest his reader. Such being the case, it was pointless to dwell upon

103

scenes of violent action when what was of real significance went on in the *minds* of the participants. Indeed, too violent a display of physical force might have specific disadvantages. Interest might be restricted to the action itself, at the expense of its deeper implications. In addition, actions that were too extraordinary jeopardized the reader's relation to the work; he escaped from his "self" into the imagined world, instead of involving his "self" in the projected conflicts and tensions. On the other hand, if surface action could be reduced to a minimum, the artist would be free to give his attention to the minds of his characters and to contrive a drama that would ensnare the minds of his readers.

Since he was dedicated to the drama of the consciousness, James had to face the problem of making what surface action he did employ count for as much as possible. Each detail had to bear some weight of significance. This involved arrranging material in such a way as to stimulate an active examination by the reader. As many as possible "fine, shy vibrations" of his characters' minds had to be presented in such a way that the reader would respond to them. To achieve this end, James employed several artistic devices. His use of supernatural elements, of deliberate ambiguity, and of a sense of the past are particularly representative of his use of these devices. They are especially suitable for discussion here because James has discussed them at considerable length himself, and they are highly illustrative of his effort to place the center of interest in the mind, the feelings, the general aesthetic awareness of his characters.

When James first used a ghostly element in his stories, he did so in a more or less traditional manner. *A Romance of Certain Old Clothes* (1868) makes use of a supernatural effect at the very end where Viola is found dead upon the floor before a forbidden chest of clothes. "Her lips were parted in entreaty, in dismay, in agony; and on her bloodless brow and cheeks there glowed the marks of ten hideous wounds from two vengeful ghostly hands." The nature of Viola's offense is as explicit as her punishment; the reader need supply nothing from his imagination. *DeGrey,* published the same year, takes place in America and has Americans as its characters, but it is saturated with old-world romance, even to including a mysterious Catholic priest and a strange curse to the effect that DeGrey brides would die shortly after their marriage.

There is a romantic air about these stories that prevents any felt response on the reader's part. They bear little testimony to James's opinion expressed three years earlier that a good ghost story should be "connected at a hundred points with the common objects of life," or with his additional, foreshadowing observation that with the old poets the dramatic interest of crime "lay in the fact that it compromised the criminal's moral repose."

The Ghostly Rental, although it appeared first in 1876, is far inferior to the kind of work James was doing at that time and was very likely written much earlier. *The Last of the Valerii* (1874) is markedly improved over the preceding stories in its treatment of the supernatural element. Still, it remains a romance; the superabundant Roman moonlight and ghostly goings-on, while they may be entertaining, do little to trouble the moral repose of either the characters or the reader.

James did not return to the use of a supernatural element until the 1890's. Many things might have stimulated his renewed interest in the possibilities of the ghost-story, but one which cannot be ignored is his brother William's interest in the supernatural. Much to the annoyance of many of his contemporary psychologists and philosophers, William James refused to rule out the possibility that supernatural forces of one kind or another actually do manifest themselves from time to time in the affairs of men. He took an active part in psychical research, and in 1890 he wrote a report on the famous medium, Mrs. Piper, for the Society for Psychical Research. The paper was read to the society in London by Henry James, who was familiar with his brother's activities on behalf of the supernatural and was no doubt in sympathy with them. From 1894 through 1896 William James was president of the Society for Psychical Research. This was the decade when Henry James most frequently employed a supernatural element in his stories.

James used a supernatural element in his mature work without any attempt to "explain" its presence on rational grounds. While supernatural interventions take place in the course of otherwise normal human experience, James accounts for the supernatural element neither through the conventional denouement of explanatory coincidence, nor by resort to the "scientific" explanation which was in vogue during the last half of the century, especially as a result of the influence of sensation novelists such as Wilkie Collins. The first of James's mature efforts, *Sir Edmund Orme* (1891), presents a well-tailored ghost who walks abroad in the sober light of day. He behaves like the most proper of mortals. It is the consciousness of the mother wherein the interest of the story centers, and the reader finds little that is farfetched in the psychological realism of the story. As in most cases in James's mature work, the ghostly element here may be linked with some unusual, even abnormal, psychological condition. This suggests a comparison with William James's investigation of psychical matters as a legitimate extension of his interest in abnormal psychology and psychopathology.

James's primary concern in his ghost-stories was not with any exposition of the supernatural; he concentrated emphasis not upon the ghost but upon the consciousness that reacted to it. The reader, presumably, was one of these, and was expected to be

galvanized from an apathetic, habitual response to a felt awareness of his impressions and of the intensified emotional tone of
the experience. Just as a spot of color upon a canvas is modified
by the succeeding spots of color applied by the artist, achieving
an entirely different value in the context of the work of art from
its value in isolation, so James modified the supernatural element in his stories. He supplied it with a humanizing substance
and form; he borrowed from it a leaven for the emotional quality of his work. Sir Edmund Orme, Peter Quint and Miss Jessel
of *The Turn of the Screw*, and "the third person" from the story
of that name are offered to the reader with all the visual detail
of their shape, costume, and manner. Spencer Brydon's *alter ego*
in *The Jolly Corner* is a vividly felt presence long before his appearance in the hallway, splendidly arrayed in evening clothes,
his face ineffectually masked by his hands, one of which had lost
two fingers.

Sometimes James's ghosts do not appear in the story at all and
are dealt with by implication. At other times the supernatural
force is not invoked until the very end, where it brings about a
suspenseful climax. Such is the case in *Nona Vincent, Owen
Wingrave, The Friends of the Friends,* and in *The Ghostly
Rental,* where, after a false ghost has held sway, a true apparition
enters—Captain Diamond's ghost, standing as Spencer Brydon's
ghost was to appear in *The Jolly Corner,* "In the hall, at the foot
of the stairs."

The supernatural element is felt still more indirectly in other
stories: as a force protesting the publication of certain papers in
Sir Dominick Ferrand and *The Real Right Thing*; and as the
phantasm of a fixed idea in *The Great Good Place, Maud-Evelyn*
and *The Beast in the Jungle.* In all of these stories, the mystic,
undefinable force is caught up in some aesthetically perceptible
form that makes a strong impression, and this impression is in-

tensely received by one or more characters. Even when the narrative includes a sensuously real ghost, James relies for his effect upon a vivid depiction of someone's felt reaction to it.

As in all James's stories, the human experience, human behavior during some critical period, is the thing of paramount concern and not the ghostly element. Consequently, it would be an artistic mistake to dwell upon the ghostly element. James found that just a slight injection of the supernatural was more effective as a force of violence than "detectives or pirates or other splendid desperadoes," since so very little of it could provoke so great an amount of intricate and subtle response. The mere appearance of a ghost, the very suggestion of an alien presence was all the novelist needed for his drama of the consciousness. The human element was the one that had to be convincingly felt by the reader. "The extraordinary is most extraordinary in that it happens to you and me, and it's of value (of value for others) but so far as visibly brought home to us."

The elaborate pageantry that attends the celebration of the Mass, the generous embellishment of Old Testament stories, and the moving accounts of miracles testify to the part aesthetically conceived supernatural elements can play in assisting belief. It is doubtful if the story of Jonah would have enjoyed such enthusiastic popularity, if it were not so delightfully told with an unabashed demand upon the "blest faculty of wonder." In this very joy of a mystified state, in the story for its own sake, James found the source and law of many of his ghost stories. He recognized the desire of the imagination for the wondrous and mystifying as an appetite that could be best assuaged through the sensuous qualities of art. A ghostly element, however vague or complex, would be accepted by the reader if it were vouched for in terms of a human, felt response. James considered this willingness on the part of readers to forego intellectual, philosophic, rational, scientific "proof" as a kind of divine gift to the artist, something upon which he could depend, "as on a strange passion planted in the heart of man for his benefit, a mysterious provision made for him in the scheme of nature."

Sometimes James coupled his use of a ghost with ambiguities carefully devised to make the reader's task a more challenging one and to require him to put forth considerable effort in order to understand the story. The kind of material he chose to deal with called for both penetration and energetic personal involvement. He found that situations very difficult to handle were the ones which eventually proved most rewarding. As the years passed, his predilection for difficult material increased until it seemed that only the difficult interested him. Difficulties provided resistance, and the greater the resistance, the greater was the demand upon the felt awareness required to cope successfully with it. To commence a work of art was, in this view, always to face a new challenge and not to resort to proven formulae.

James tried to draw from the reader of his work a response similar to his own reaction to the subject-matter. Through a judicious use of such a device as ambiguity, he attempted to stimulate the reader to a sensitive, thorough awareness of his impressions. He did not want to *tell* the reader the significance of things, because by so doing he would place the reader in a passive role; the reader's attention would not be as alert, he would not have his own felt perception of subtleties, make his own precise discriminations and have his personal sense of the evolving interrelations. In short, the reader's consciousness would have little part in the drama. All the rewards he ought to gain—and would normally gain through close attention at a play—would be lost if he did not pay close attention to the novel.

The novels James wrote during his major phase require a large expanse of time to unfold properly and to assert their tone. It is only after he has viewed several scenes that the reader begins to comprehend the real nature of the characters and to grasp the issues at stake. For full appreciation, he must have a sense of personal involvement, have his own funded experience shaken out of apathy and brought to bear on the action. Ambiguity was appropriate for achieving these ends because the reader recognized it as a familiar thing in his life, "one of the very sharpest of the realities," and knew what it meant in terms of aroused curiosity, sensitivity, imagination.

One of James's most widely read stories, *The Turn of the Screw,* is heavily dependent upon ambiguity for its effectiveness. Since James was not concerned with conveying an intellectual idea, but with effecting an intense experience for his readers, the exact nature of the evil in the story is left unspecified. James saw it as his problem to involve the reader in the aesthetically vivid situation with a sense of brooding, menacing disaster. From that point, he reasoned, the reader's imagination would supply any missing specifications. The measure of James's success here may be judged by the large number of critical articles that have been printed offering to explain the nature of the evil in *The Turn of the Screw.* The story may almost be used as an index of critical techniques and of shifting fashions in evil.

While there can be no doubt that most of James's centers of consciousness are remarkable for their intelligence, it is also evident that he constantly displays them in a condition of incertitude, examining motives, weighing possibilities, unsure of just which course would be the best to take. The reader, James hoped, would struggle along with these central figures and try to make the correct interpretations, supply missing links, make the right decisions. Too much intelligence, he recognized, could be disastrous for the illusion he wished to achieve. The reader would not feel a similarity between his own and the characters' liability to error and confusion.

As an artist, James grouped his contextually relevant material from a prolonged observation of life. His purpose was to present one unified episode of experience in each work of art. He did not dwell upon the lives of his characters beyond this experience through an account of how their money had been earned, where they had been educated, or other irrelevant circumstances. The very ambiguity in which James shrouds certain aspects of his characters contributes toward an illusion of continuity between the novel and life. It is as though he expected the reader to say, once he had been given a few glimpses of the character, "Yes, I know the kind of person you mean"; as though he assumed the reader was in a position to compare, and could be trusted to supply antecedents—and on occasion an aftermath—from his own experience.

To many readers, the conclusion of *The Portrait of a Lady* seems no conclusion at all. It appears, for one thing, that Isabel Archer has even graver crises impending than those she has just survived. James anticipated this criticism and jotted this reply in his notebook, "The *whole* of anything is never told; you can only take what groups together. What I have done has that unity—it groups together. It is complete in itself—and the rest may be taken up or not, later." When the reader turns from the drama staged in Isabel Archer's consciousness, he must realize that many of the elements that were poised in tension there are still unresolved in the society of which he is a part. It is possible to see in *The Portrait of a Lady* a composite of mirrored aspects of the world. Grouped together are reflections of life in New England, England, and Italy; of business, social, and artistic interests; of the very old and the very young. A detailed account of these aspects would have swelled enormously the size of the book, but, other considerations aside, it is very doubtful if the realism of the story would have been increased. The very absence of detailed specification makes it easier for the reader to accept Isabel Archer's experience as part of general human experience and hence something in which he shares.

There would be little or no defense for ambiguity in a work of art if its presence were due to carelessness or caprice. It would be even more objectionable if it happened to frustrate the proper development of the work, or to becloud material that should be explicit. Even when ambiguity was employed deliberately for an artistic purpose, James believed the reader should always feel that some general ideas are present. He recognized that because of the unique combination of elements forming an individual identity, each reader would have somewhat different reactions to the same work of art. Yet he wanted each reader to involve his identity in the successive crises of the novel, and it was the artist's obligation to maintain a consistent, organic development of his material and thereby justify the reader's good faith. It would be as much of a betrayal of the reader to impose pointless difficulties as it would be to impose an arbitrary solution on the difficulties raised.

The existence of ambiguities under such conditions that they incite the reader to scrutinize carefully several possible modes of action, or to evaluate moral subtleties as never before, struck James as one of the finest elements a novel could possess. James had little relish for works of art that made a quick, popular success through their clever restatement of simple, familiar material. An ever-hungry public soon exhausted the offering and cast it aside. Great art could be visited again and again, offering its admirer with each visit meanings that had somehow eluded perception before. The alterations brought about in each person's awareness through the passage of time also made it possible repeatedly to experience something new from great art. James never found life to be simple and the same; he found that close attention and careful discrimination inevitably brought out subtleties and complexities. Art had to imitate life in its amplitude and suggestiveness, to make room for the exercise of the imagination and to avoid the kind of obvious and definitive qualities that put an end to the searching activity in the reader's mind.

Just as James used a ghostly element or ambiguity from time to time, so he occasionally invoked a sense of the past in his work as a means of effecting a drama of the consciousness. Here, again, it was a case of getting a maximum amount of felt response in return for a minimum of external action. The sudden, brief moment of vision in which the artist feels himself confronted with some important truth, James would contend, is only apparently spontaneous. For in order to respond feelingly to the impression, the artist had to bring to bear upon it some meaning that had already been evolving in his mind. A landscape, a building, a person, a phrase overheard by chance are of worth to the artist, not in isolation, but as a nexus of meanings that extend back into the past. James considered that the artist needed to recognize that his material was rooted in the past, not only his personal past, but the past of a race or nation, and that he should provide for this condition in his work.

James had no veneration of the past for its own sake. His appreciation of the highly evolved forms of European religious, social, and artistic life was not a sterile antiquarianism. These aspects of European life spoke directly to his sensuous imagination as concrete images reflecting the complex and powerful influences shaping society about him. In England, he found, every contact seemed to expose the interrelation of the English mind with the past. The artist had but to move about England and observe, to acquire the key to the English mind. English traditions, institutions, habits, attitudes, standards, all of which were in some form sensibly displayed, seemed to have been intuitively absorbed by the English mind. The formative process was long and complex, and it took a long time to acquire an understanding of the final product, but James considered the effort worth while.

One of the reasons James found the American scene difficult to deal with was that its brief past had been embodied in so few visible forms. On one occasion, William Dean Howells objected to James's extensive use of Old World settings, traditions and the rest as "dreary and worn-out paraphernalia." James replied to him, "It is on manners, customs, usages, habits, forms, upon all these things matured and established that a novelist lives—they are the very stuff his work is made of; and in saying that in the absence of those 'dreary and worn-out paraphernalia' which I enumerate as being wanting in American society, 'we have simply the whole of human life left,' you beg (to my sense) the question. I should say we had just so much less of it as these same 'paraphernalia' represent, and I think they represent an enormous quantity of it." Howells' use of the term "paraphernalia" with its suggestion that the material alluded to was extrinsic to human experience indicates his fundamental divergence from James's position. To James, manners, traditions and the rest were far more significant as clues to the nature of a culture than the unformed, naive expressions of behavior that Howells praised. Manners, customs and the rest represented what man had made of himself over a period of time; they represented an organized, purposeful effort in social living.

Just how an inadequate sense of the past could affect art is suggested in the review of Howells' work published by James in 1886. James thought that both in substance and form, Howells had been too content with what readily presented itself to his eye and hand. He had great praise for certain qualities in Howells' work, but found it in general too concerned with the common, the immediate, the familiar, the colloquial, the paltry. At bottom, James objected to Howells' failure to provide for any drama of the consciousness. There was little challenge to the mind, and the perspective of life enshrined in Howells' work seemed very local and temporary. Even in his personal life, it seemed to James that the manners and customs Howells subscribed to acted to cut him off from life, rather than to promote a healthy and natural social intercourse for him. He was the prototype of Strether in *The Ambassadors* before his visit to Paris, when the provincial community of "Woollett" prescribed his conduct in the world.

James's autobiographical volume, *The Middle Years*, remarks that one of the most important aspects of his trip to England in the year 1869 was his contact with the enormous multiplicity of reference which enveloped European life. It was something he had been but slightly aware of before, and in comparison with London life the previous solutions seemed thin. James was anything but a "passionate pilgrim"; his early reviews and letters indicate that he was sharply critical of English life and literature. But the aesthetic richness of the scene fascinated him because it made the past seem so close. "I delight in a palpable imaginable *visitable* past . . . in which the precious element of closeness, telling so of connexions but tasting so of differences, remains appreciable." James often tried to incorporate this same suggestion of differences in his novels, especially through characters connected with aristocratic families. Part of Strether's grand illumination is his sensitivity to Madame de Vionnet's historical connections.

In his short story *The Birthplace* (1903), James ridicules a perverted respect for the past, the kind of fetishism that makes a shrine out of some poet's home or otherwise venerates objects associated with someone of great artistic repute. Pilgrims to such shrines, it seemed to him, had little sense of the dead man's work; they were not trying to live back into the conditions out of which it had found expression. For them, a spurious birthplace would suffice, particularly if their visit was enlivened by a romantic account of the great man's life.

But certain places and things did embody a spiritual value for James. They had been created as the expression of the needs, spiritual and social, of certain communities or certain individuals and had absorbed associations from successive generations. Through aesthetic perception of these places and things, James considered it possible to experience, to some extent, the conditions that had given them birth. He found that the process of exploring the past this way was a deeply personal experience, requiring calm and long periods of time for the spell to work. White-Mason, in *Crapy Cornelia* (1909), discovered that if he was to recover anything from his life, it was by making it over, re-creating it with the help of Cornelia Rasch, a woman who had managed to live outside the terrible rush of modern life. Together they would explore their lost world.

The sense of the past is of a piece with the rest of James's art in that it works to make the reader perceive his experience and to wrest what is beautiful and meaningful from the hurly-burly. It is for this reason that Clement Searle, in *A Passionate Pilgrim* (1871), and Frank Granger, in *Flickerbridge* (1902), withdraw from busy city life to fine old country-houses, where they have access to a "visitable past." Mrs. Gracedew, in *Covering End* (1898), feels acutely the necessity of preserving old estates and other material things that have the tone of time. She argues, " 'We share the poor fate of humanity whatever we

do, and we do something to help and console when we've something precious to show. What on earth is more precious than
what the ages have slowly wrought? They've trusted us, in such
a case, to keep it—to do something, in our turn, for *them* . . .
It's such a virtue, in anything, to have lasted; it's such an
honour, for anything, to have been spared. To all strugglers
from the wreck of time hold out a pitying hand!' " The emphasis placed here upon the shared fate as well as the shared obligation of humanity is further insisted upon. " 'This *is* the temple—
don't profane it! Keep up the old altar kindly—you can't set
up a new one as good. You *must* have beauty in your life, don't
you see?—that's the only way to make sure of it for the lives of
others.' " Here, as elsewhere when he provides for the sense of
the past, James sounds a note of his alliance with the meta-
physicals of English literature through his sense of the continuity and community of human relationships underlying the
apparent isolation of the individual. It is especially evident in
this capacity to perceive aesthetically, through the objects and
forms of daily life, the immanence of past and present generations.

In *The Sense of the Past,* James observed how art enabled an
individual to recover a past moment as a present experience,
permitting him to breathe as other men had breathed, to feel
the pressures they had felt. By way of enriching the drama of
the consciousness, the artist could secure notes of truth in this
respect that were beyond the scope of history. He could supply
the kind of evidence, in short, "for which there had never been
documents enough, or for which documents mainly, however
multiplied, would never *be* enough." As with a ghostly element
or a skillfully contrived ambiguity, James could interest his
reader in an aesthetic surface and then lead him to an exploration of "the interest behind the interest."

In a sense, economy was the watchword that directed all of James's devices such as those discussed above. They occupied a minimal portion of the novel's surface, but their effect was far reaching on the reader's mind. James was haunted by the necessity to express as much of his subject as he possibly could, and this necessity conflicted inevitably with the limitations on length imposed by editors. The vital things had to be said, the deepest feelings aroused, in the most concise way. The great stretches of his work, he recognized, had to be devoted to the search for meanings, to someone's effort to understand and be aware. The devices James conceived in his effort to place the drama in the consciousness of his characters and of his readers proved highly successful and are among his finest contributions to the technical resources of modern writers.

All life therefore comes back to the question of our speech, the medium through which we communicate with each other. These relations are made possible, are registered, are verily constituted, by our speech, and are successful (to repeat my word) in proportion as our speech is worthy of its great human and social function; is developed, delicate, flexible, rich—an adequate accomplished fact. The more it suggests and expresses the more we live by it—the more it promotes and enhances life. Its quality, its authenticity, its security, are hence supremely important for the general multifold opportunity, for the dignity and integrity of our existence. James, The Question of Our Speech (1905).

8

The Prose Medium

SPEECH WAS ONE OF THE CHIEF GLORIES OF THE HOUSEHOLD IN which Henry James grew up. With the exception of Mrs. James, who functioned as audience and arbiter, the members of the family were intensely vocal. If the head of the household, Henry James, Sr., had pronounced "views" on the topics of the day, so did his sons and daughter, and debate constantly raged. Dinner-guests have written of their alarm, when exuberant little Jameses gesticulated with knives and forks at one another, in heated defense of their ideas. Age enjoyed no privilege in the domestic arena; it was a sheer survival of the fittest with victory going to the one who could most nimbly work on the feelings as well as the minds of his audience.

From speaking to writing was an easy transition for most members of the family. Henry James, Sr. talked a great deal about his ideas, then he wrote them down in much the same manner he had talked about them, and, finally, he read what he had written to his wife to see if it sounded right. William James, also, wrote very much as he spoke in utter disregard of prevailing literary styles in psychology and philosophy. He gave color and texture to the general and abstract and sent them skipping through his pages. As the children grew up, they acquired friends far and near to whom they wrote incessantly, and this practice further bridged the gap between speaking and writing. When members of the family were apart, they kept in touch with one another by means of frequent letters, often of extraordinary length and remarkable grace.

As a child, Henry James listened to his father read from his works on theology, and although he had little notion of what they were about, he was charmed by many passages that carried a strong sensuous appeal. Many of the images his father used were interesting *as* images, so much so that as images alone they persisted in James's memory, while the abstract argument was lost. He characterized his father's style as ". . . too philosophic for life, and at the same time too living . . . for thought." It is significant that at an early age James was critical of the aesthetic value of prose, and he notes, in regard to his father's work, "I heard it, felt it, saw it, both shamefully enjoyed and shamefully denied it as form, though as form only. . . ."

James's taste for a prose that appealed to his senses found gratification in writers close at hand, such as Emerson and Thoreau, and it also led him to qualify carefully his praise of such a writer as Hawthorne. When he came to write a partial portrait of Emerson, James dwelled upon that writer's sensitivity to natural things and offered quotations to illustrate his ability to capture the sparkle of nature. At the same time he described Thoreau as one who wrote ". . . beautiful pages, which read like a translation of Emerson into the sounds of the field and forest and which no one who has ever loved nature in New

England, or indeed anywhere, can fail to love. . . ." The capacity of these men to express their often complex thought in a prose that was richly sensuous did not fail, then, to make its mark on James.

His sensitivity to the absence of this quality in Hawthorne's work is equally of note. When James wrote his study of Hawthorne in 1879, he attacked *The Scarlet Letter* because the characters did not come alive. They remained artificial figures arranged to depict a state of mind. Interest centered not in the people, but in the abstract situation. At times, it seemed to James, the symbolism of the story was mechanical, overdone, almost trivial. By the time he wrote this biography, James's awareness of the possibilities of prose as an aesthetic medium had been greatly heightened through his contact with the French novelists and a prolonged study of their work.

James tried allegory himself, in *Benvolio* (1875), where he is guilty of all the faults he attributes to Hawthorne, and in *The Author of Beltraffio* (1884), where he demonstrated that he could write successful allegory. There is a successful fusion of image and idea in the later work. The quality James most admired in Hawthorne's writings, the exploration beyond appearances to underlying moral meanings, was something that became highly characteristic of his own work. But while both men constantly sifted their experience for a deeper meaning, Hawthorne's thought was inclined to abstract ideas from his experience and concentrate on a manipulation of these ideas, leaving the sensuous images to operate as a kind of pantomime. James, on the other hand, kept his impressions constantly in mind and thought in terms of a succession of dramatic scenes. Hawthorne relied most heavily upon the reader's intellect, while James relied upon the reader's "felt" response. James had little use for allegory by the time he came to write his biography of Hawthorne. It seemed to him to be too much an intellectual game and to deny aesthetic value. He wanted to fashion a prose medium that had a rich sensuous surface and, when he used symbols, wanted to make them aesthetically vivid and yet organically related to the whole substance of the work of art.

During his early years, James had every respect for abstract ideas and formal logic. When his personal impressions were at odds with scientific theory, he deferred to science. But abstractions and theories never made any important impression upon him. He was impressed by things seen, heard, felt, and in turn he tried progressively in his writing to impress his readers via their senses. His criticism rapidly became the record of his personal response to literature, written in an informal, if highly cultivated, style and couched in very figurative language.

From the first he had had the habit of absorbing his thoughts and feelings into a palpable symbol. *A Small Boy and Others* records an experience that occurred during a visit to Europe when James was but a child. It involved little that was extraordinary, simply a ruined tower and a peasant woman clad in a black bodice, a white shirt and a red petticoat. But this woman called to his mind everything that reading, conversation and travel had previously suggested to him about Europe. She was a synthesis of all that meant "Europe," and as such was to remain in his mind and serve as a bridge to many other things. This early impression suggests James's later practice of finding a sensuous embodiment for the most vaguely defined ideas. It did not matter how complex or indefinite they were; working always in terms of aesthetic impressions, he was able to conjure up a symbol for them, one with a strong aesthetic appeal. Although an idea might be interlaced with sensitive, intricate meanings, he could weave it masterfully into the aesthetic pattern of his prose.

In James's latest work it is by no means always possible to say just what symbolic significance any particular thing or action might have, because the meaning is qualified by the work as a whole as it evolves. A specific symbol which has a reasonably definite, "extractable" meaning at one point, may have a different meaning at some other point in the novel. It is the very amplitude of their suggestiveness that gives enduring value to many of James's works. A narrow, specialized range of meanings attaching to the narrow, specialized social class that provides the immediate setting of so much of his work would very likely have doomed it by now.

The most diverse things could take on symbolic value for James. Often it was the room in which a certain person lived, or his clothes, or ornaments; sometimes it was a pair of glasses, some letters, a painting or some other work of art. The titles of several of his novels are enough to suggest a symbolic value that pervades the entire story: *The Madonna of the Future, The Golden Bowl, The Death of the Lion,* and *The Figure in the Carpet,* for example. In each case meaning has been absorbed into a sensory image from the whole context of the story. As a result, James's symbols have validity only in the context in which they occur. They do not have an iconic or indexical value, nor are they conventional, traditional signs with a generally accepted meaning. The symbol, as employed by James, contributes to the essential value of prose as a medium. To the extent that a symbol or other image *expressed* an idea, it *was* that idea, James insisted, and any attempt to separate the idea from its symbol or vice versa was impossible. In this way prose was a "medium," like paint, or marble, or sound, through which the artist expressed his subject matter, and not simply a "means," like a formula or legal phrase, that served merely as a convenient forceps in the delivery of abstract ideas.

James's belief that an idea and the expression of it were one and the same had as its corollary that this expression should be as full as possible. Despite the length of his works and his constant habit of expanding an idea beyond his anticipations of its possibilities, James's prose medium is characterized by intension rather than extension. It is a prose that compresses as much meaning as possible into each word. It attempts to sustain a steady flow of concrete imagery. Through foreshortening, multiple reference, symbolic structure, and every device that came to his hand, James tried to avoid "looseness." "The explosive principle" in the artist's material, he observed, should alone be allowed to develop, and everything not of the essence should be discarded.

It was, in part, this desire for a tightly packed prose medium, a surface iridescent because of the amount that gleamed through, and the contempt for "looseness," that motivated James's meticulous attention to detail. He analyzed situations tirelessly and with precision, tried to find out exactly wherein lay the appeal of a character, the charm of a scene. William James stated in his *Psychology* that a man's thinking depended upon the things he experienced, but that his habits of attention largely determined what these should be. On the basis of this principle Henry James pleaded with writers, critics and the general public to give scrupulous attention to every detail of the prose medium.

A close critical attention to writing made the reader aware of what was pleasing and nourishing to his mind. This, in turn, caused him to search out the most satisfactory writing and, in effect, to search out the reasons why it was the most satisfactory. James called this process "the very education of our imaginative life." As a result of such education, the reader—or critic, or artist, since one was but a more developed stage of the other, in James's opinion—came to know how to refine and what refined most. He became liberated from chance and mere instinct; he was able to take a hand in providing his own satisfaction and in opening the door to the great flood of awareness.

As a splendid example of what could be accomplished by the right kind of attention to the prose medium, James pointed to Flaubert. One of Flaubert's most annoying problems had been that of trying to fashion a prose of elegance out of the French language. Its sheer sounds seemed to rebuff the results demanded by his sense of taste. Also, the elements of language had so to be selected and combined as to comply with exacting principles of rhythm and harmony. The kind of expression he desired depended upon successful manipulation of these basic components of language. James speculated upon what Flaubert's reaction might have been had he been confronted with the even more intractable English language, so large a percentage of which consisted of "that" and "which," "it," "to," and the auxiliaries "be," and "do." Flaubert's remarkable triumph over the difficulties posed by his medium was, James held, a challenge as well as an inspiration to American novelists.

Quite as remarkable as his gift for evaluating and handling language was Flaubert's skill at making it serve its proper function in the aesthetic whole. A phrase never was allowed to exist for its own pretty sake. James was quick to discover the carelessness of other writers in this respect. His earliest reviews had regularly taken to task writers who arbitrarily hitched chunks of description to their work, or who used words and phrases merely for some picturesque quality supposed to reside in them. He grew weary of singling out the sins of "female authors," who frequently tacked on empty expressions in the belief that they were endowing their work with beauty. Conversely, James repeatedly criticized the naturalists, who seemed on occasion to trick out their works with gratuitous bits of ugliness. He believed in the organic nature of the prose medium. Verbal elements that did not belong in the work of art were a parasitic growth, sapping the strength of the organism to which they were attached.

James was not favorably impressed by the condition of prose fiction in England toward the end of the 'eighties. "How few they are in number and how soon we could name them," he wrote, "the writers of English prose, at the present moment, the quality of whose prose is personal, expressive, renewed at each attempt." One of the writers whom he singled out as being in the elect circle of fine prose writers was Robert Louis Stevenson. ". . . He is curious of expression and regards the literary form not simply as a code of signals, but as the keyboard of a piano, and as so much plastic material. . . . He is as different as possible from the sort of writer who regards words as numbers, and a page as the mere addition of them; much more, to carry out our image, the dictionary stands for him as a wardrobe, and a preposition as a button for his coat." James's comparison here of prose to the media of the musician and painter gives the measure of his conception of the prose medium as one that appealed to perception through sensual stimuli. Just as a sonata has its meaning in the sounds of which it is composed and these sounds are not merely a bridge to some further meaning, just as the meaning of a painting is to be found in color and its arrangement on a canvas and not in some association with a "real life" scene, so the arrangement of words in a work of fiction expresses a meaning and is not simply a vehicle for communicating information.

The successive brush-strokes of the artist create the meaning of the painting even as the painting itself is created. Language has a similar creative function in prose fiction. James's awareness of the extent to which the work of art exists and grows through the artist's relation with the words themselves is very evident in his criticism and is explicit in his discussions of his own work. In his effort to find the precise words to express his thought, the artist often clarifies the thought in his own mind and recognizes finer possibilities for his fiction. From his own experience, James recognized that in the process of writing fiction there was a constant interaction between the material supplied by the mind—impressions, feelings, ideas—and the words in which he sought to express this material. The very act of organizing words effected an organization of his thoughts. Words became every bit as much elements of the substance of the work of art as they were elements of the form. *As* words, they determined what the reader should enjoy and understand, and all possible care should be given, therefore, to their selection and arrangement.

The writer of fiction had always to guard against the possibility that his work might become words only. The popularity of "dialogue" was having serious consequences for the novel in this respect, James thought. It led writers to string words together that simply added unrelated or superfluous substance to the novel and violated its form. The English, he observed, were very fond of dialogue at the theater. They admired its leanness, the sinew-and-bone compactness of a good play. But the English did not care for this same kind of dialogue in their reading. There, they tolerated all kinds of flabbiness, repetition, digression and so forth. When James proceeded to construct his own dialogue so as to have it "organic and dramatic," as tight and hard as the dialogue in a good play, he often heard the charge that it was artificial.

James was doing with his dialogue what he did with every other aspect of his work, namely, making it representative of the best in human experience. If his dialogue was improbable at times, at least he erred on the side of the angels. But James would not have conceded that the dialogue in his work was unnatural, he would have contended that it was simply refined and that readers should not complain of the absence of the usual dross.

An indication of how James would have defended, in part, his treatment of dialogue can be gained from some remarks by Gabriel Nash in *The Tragic Muse*. Nash deplored the lack of standards in the English theatre. He found that the purity of speech had been allowed to degenerate into "abominable dialects and individual tricks, any vulgarity . . ." and voiced a plea for "any style that *is* a style, that's a system, a consistency, an art, that contributes a positive beauty to utterance." What Nash wanted was called "affectation" and he accepted the term as applying to a manner of speech based upon selection, arrangement, a manner that was the fruit of prolonged, deliberate reflection. Furthermore, a cultivated style should not be considered artificial because of the degree of its separation from so-called "instinctual" speech. "The talent, the desire, the energy are an instinct; but by the time these things become a performance they're an instinct put in its place."

James's attack here on "abominable dialects" and "so-called 'instinctual' speech" must not be misinterpreted as an attack upon dialect or "instinctual" speech. The qualifying adjectives are necessary because James had every respect for dialect that is a genuinely native product and for speech that is instinctual in the sense that it has not been affected by jargons, literary turns, and especially by forces that separate a word from its roots.

The position James took on this subject emerges clearly in his discussion of why he neglected to deal with the American scene in general. The one reason that counted for most with him was that the countless items of prose fiction which did attempt to cope with the American scene testified to the tangled snarl of American speech. These works reproduced all kinds of so-called "dialects," which were not true dialects at all, but filled with unconscious echoes of different speech-patterns, popular slang, and the deadening effect of formal schooling. The writers of such works enshrined a bastard vernacular, "disinherited of the felt difference between the speech of the soil and the speech of the newspaper. . . ." James did not regret having contributed no stone to such a monument.

Since James believed that a nation's speech was a direct reflection of its culture, it follows that he considered American culture to be raw, undifferentiated, and groping its way with apparently little intelligent sense of direction. However, he felt there was a remedy for this. He held it was necessary to eliminate chance and to control as far as possible the merely instinctual development of speech. This could be achieved by examining one's experience with the utmost care, cultivating a preference for the better elements that enter into its composition, and projecting an intelligent course for future action. If democracy had cheapened language in America, it was certainly possible still to raise the general level of language if a conscious effort was made for that purpose. Americans had to pay attention to the elements that composed their speech, to give the requisite sound-value to consonants and vowels, instead of slurring them together or simply dropping them. They had to grow aware of the meanings of words and to feel a logic in grammatical patterns.

What James wanted for language in America was not an authority, nor a fixed way of doing things, but an intelligent and sensitive responsibility in the matter of language. A sense of tradition, he considered, would help to arrest the fluid looseness of form; an interest in the origins of words and of the use made of them in literature would do a great deal to promote a "manner" of speaking. He wanted a sense of the past to operate with language as with culture in general, not for the sake of learning about the past alone, but because of the immeasurable contribution it might make to the present. The place to begin was not in a book of rules, but in one's own mind, discriminating amongst the images there and selecting with care the ideal words to communicate them.

Where his own speech was concerned, James spared no effort to achieve a finished manner. He spent his lifetime examining words, listening to their sounds, inspecting their meanings, fitting them together in patterns, adjusting their rhythms, aware always of what they might do for him. By the time he was fifty, the result was a unique mode of expression that usually astonished the people who met him. The parenthetic asides, the many qualifying clauses, the endless sentences, the slow cadence, the prolonged search for the proper word—all combined to form a manner that was unlike anything heard on either side of the Atlantic.

To a considerable extent his way of speaking was a result of the practice of dictating his fiction, a practice he began about midway through the 1890's. James preferred to dictate his work because, aside from certain labor-saving advantages, it afforded him the opportunity to examine how the words sounded, how they flowed together, without having to interrupt his attention in order to put the words on paper. Similarly, when the work was finished, he preferred to have it read aloud, so that the vitality of the spoken word might be retained. Prose intended for silent reading, he believed, was a prose that tended to lose its contact with life. It became "literary," stereotyped, automatic. Prose written to be read aloud retained its relationship with living speech. To read a novel aloud, James maintained, was to test its values, to put to the proof its appeal to the imagination, "to the spiritual and the aesthetic vision." If it failed this test, it did not meet one of the necessary conditions of life.

9

It is the blessing of the art he practices that it is made up of experience conditioned, infinitely, in this personal way—the sum of the feeling of life as reproduced by innumerable natures; natures that feel through all their differences, testify through their diversities. These differences, which make the identity, are of the individual; they form the channel by which life flows through him, and how much he is able to give us of life—in other words, how much he appeals to us—depends on whether they form it solidly. James, Introduction to Kipling's Soldiers Three *(1891).*

The Personal Equation

JAMES'S APPRENTICESHIP AS A WRITER WAS SIMILAR TO THAT OF many other writers in that he first sought to imitate well-established novelists and then, progressively, evolved his personal idiom. But where James differed sharply from most of the writers of his day and from those who followed him was in the extent to which he deliberately cultivated his personal expression of things. Victorian novelists in general tended to reproduce similar plot-situations; familiar character-types met the usual difficulties and resolved them in a fairly predictable way. The exponents of naturalism, who were very much to the fore by the end of the century, brought to the novel a vast catalogue of items that had previously been omitted. The "new" novelists, like their predecessors, said a great many things that were worth saying about human nature and social conditions. But like their predecessors they, too, were usually content to portray characters in conflict with the accepted framework of values that existed around them. The artist knew where he stood; he felt assured in his knowledge of his own character and could

132

proceed upon reasonably well established principles with regard to general human nature in writing his novel.

It is clear from James's observations upon his art that he proceeded with no such assurance of certain certainties. Rather, he viewed the human situations that provided him with his *données* as problems to which no conventional system of moral algebra could be applied. Each problem required a separate inspection. The more difficulties the problem posed the better, because in the sensitive process of analysis, a process that could take several years, James found that he made illuminating discoveries about his experience as well as about his own nature. He described the act of writing fiction as an "act of life," and it was an act that was creative in two ways: it created a work of art that bore in every part the evidence of his personal sense of things, and as a result of the deep, intense probing of his personal values, it inevitably created afresh his ethical ideal and its claims upon his self-identity. After the experience of *The Wings of the Dove,* he could indeed say with Kate Croy, "We shall never be again as we were!"

At the bottom of many of James's ideas can be found the common element of his belief in the essential importance of the individual. In criticism he sought the critic's personal, felt response to literature, and it was because he found such a large measure of this quality in the work of Matthew Arnold and Sainte-Beuve that he admired them. He sought always in fiction to possess himself of each writer's particular "window," the unique vantage point from which that writer regarded life. James treasured a sense of the past because, in part, it enabled him to share the differing perspectives of men who belonged to another age. In *The Altar of the Dead* he protested against a dense, materialistic society, wedded to the immediate and finite, that allowed death to cut off callously the fine awareness of individual personality.

The characters in James's fiction are often in opposition to the forces in modern society that do not recognize any necessity to preserve moral integrity. Isabel Archer's respect for the marriage vow, the sacredness Fleda Vetch attaches to the engagement bond, Lambert Strether's conviction that he must not personally gain anything from his embassage all seem far-fetched only when the preservation of moral integrity is considered of lesser value than "the pursuit of happiness." In each case James has struggled with the problem of self-identity and has come through with the solution that, whatever renunciation may be involved, these characters must act in the way they do if the complex of values which constitutes their moral personality is not to be violated.

James's refusal to be satisfied with the surface character of individuals and his insistence upon diving into complicated moral depths is directly connected with his effort to salvage the "person." This effort draws its strength from his view of the world as material for change. It was his opinion that the artist can regard the world with reference to what he would like it to be. James not only attacked the naturalistic novel on the ground that its selection of material was highly arbitrary, that it presented only the worst aspects of human behavior, but he also opposed its determinism. In electing to present "the other side of the coin," James took full cognizance of evil and ugly aspects of life, but chose to expend his talent on emphasizing an ethical ideal. He wrote of Zola's *La Joie de Vivre*, ". . . granting the nature of the curiosity and the substance laboured in, the patience is again prodigious, but which makes us wonder what pearl of philosophy, of suggestion or just of homely recognition, the general picture, as of rats dying in a hole, has to offer."

Such a writer as Zola, James would argue, must have had some sense of a better way of life in order to react so violently against the sordidness he encountered. However rare his glimpses of the finer state of things might have been, they were still just as real as the familiar vulgarities. How much better, it seemed to James, to explore one's reaction against evil and ugliness and present the "possible other case." The artist could shape from his own moral reaction a transforming ideal and make the experience afforded by his art an ennobling one. Since the artist is free to shape his material as he sees fit, it seemed much better to James for him to dwell upon those qualities he valued most in himself than to dwell upon those which tended to equate him with animals. James recognized a capacity in man to reorder his existence, to shape his conduct and his values in accord with a chosen ethos.

James's plea to artists that they should give their personal sense of things in their work was not a plea for "self-expression" as that term is generally understood. He did not try to express his "self" but to express those of his impressions which bore some relation to human culture and were of general interest and significance. This process amounted to self-expression, perhaps, but it was far different from the disordered emotionalism usually comprehended by that term. As James pondered the relation between the artist and his art, it seemed to him that the latter was worth while in direct proportion to the extent it embodied each artist's unique vision of life.

James's desire that the artist should stress the finer aspect of human conduct was not at all incompatible with his conviction that the artist should be true to all of his experience. He believed that the question was one of selection, treatment, and emphasis. These factors had inevitably to operate, and James found it grotesque that they should operate so overwhelmingly in favor of the ugly. Too often artists were not true to their feelings, the moral truth indicated by their reactions, when they reproduced hideous characters and settings. They were being true to the conditions that brought about the impression and neglecting the really important matter of the impression itself.

If James had not had his belief in the need for each artist to choose and express his own subject matter, he might have found it easier to accept the manner in which society interfered to prescribe what material was suitable for artistic treatment. As it was, he bitterly resented society's intrusion into the matter. He repeatedly set forth his position. In "The Art of Fiction," he complained that there was an unfortunate discrepancy between that which the people knew and that which they would admit to knowing, between that which they felt to be a part of life and that which they would allow to enter into literature. The so-called "moral purpose" which was presumed to be exhibited in the English novel by restricting subject matter to topics acceptable for adolescents impressed James as quite the reverse of an accomplishment in the field of morals. "The essence of moral energy," he wrote, "is to survey the whole field."

The position James takes on the relation of morality to art in "The Art of Fiction" is a development of his idea of a "moral sense." He had early distinguished between the practice of moralizing and the operation of a moral element in the novel. It was not until he approached his major phase, however, that he stopped searching for a "moral sense," *per se,* in the novel and came to regard the moral quality of the work as an inseparable aspect of the artist's personal awareness.

From this viewpoint, no work of art could have a deep moral

quality unless its producer had a correspondingly deep moral sense. The same applied to the artistic stature of a work of art; it would correspond to the artistic sense of the artist. The moral sense and the artistic sense lay very close together in that ". . . the deepest quality of a work of art will always be the quality of the mind of the producer." The operation of the moral sense as well as the artistic sense was intuitive, spontaneous. James pointed out that individuals such as Hawthorne, Emerson, Charles Eliot Norton and William Wetmore Story persistently displayed the nature of their spiritual ancestry when they were most concerned with art. Even when they tried to lose themselves in the labyrinth of delight, they held fast to the clue of duty. Turgenieff's work is pervaded by his moral sense, and his work offered to James ". . . a capital example of moral meaning giving a sense to form and form giving relief to moral meaning."

Work such as Turgenieff's illustrated for James that the only way to communicate moral ideas in fiction is to communicate them as an intrinsic part of the experience provided the reader by the novel. If there were no concern with the moral aspects of life guiding the author in his first perception of the *donnée*, in his reflection upon it, and in his expression of it, there could be no reason to expect moral value as part of the final effect. If the vision of the author and the pressure of his will were conditioned by a moral sense, the finished work would embody a moral quality aesthetically, and it would be offered to the reader with all the added power and beauty effected by art.

Conflicts involving moral values are easily among the most profound in human experience, and art can communicate such conflicts. But this is only possible, according to James, when the mind of the artist is capable of piercing the superficial and misleading to seize upon what he can recognize as true and beautiful. Laws, customs, all *a priori* guides are of only incidental value in such a search. James relished those situations wherein it was exceedingly difficult to distinguished right from wrong. In the course of resolving such a predicament, he took pains on several occasions to illustrate the inadequacy of judgments based on predetermined positions. The final court of appeal, to his mind, was what may be described as the conscience, aided with every resource of the reflective intelligence. It was the nature of the individual that counted.

A failure to appreciate the nature of the relationship between the artist and his work was one of the most serious charges James brought against the advocates of "art for art's sake." It seemed to him that they displayed a marked provincialism of spirit, in contrast to their assumed culture, when they spoke of morality and art as though the former were something one could add to, or keep out of, the latter at will. James contended that moral quality had everything to do with the importance of a work of art, and that it was impossible to decide arbitrarily to keep this quality out of a work of art or to insert it. There could be no doubt, he averred, of what the great artists would say on this matter. "People of that temper feel that the whole thinking man is one . . ."

The contention that each artist should express his view of life in his own way, imparting to it the fullest measure of his individual quality, assumed a primary importance for James toward the close of the century when he determined to allow himself all the stylistic freedom the expression of his material required. He had sincere and enthusiastic admiration for the widely differing styles of many of his contemporaries. The more their writing bore the impress of their personality, indeed, the more he treasured it, for this gave him a greater opportunity to extend the range of his own experience. One of the reasons why James felt so keenly H. G. Wells's parody of him (*Boon*) was that it seemed to indicate that Wells had been totally unable to accept the conditions of James's personal viewpoint, that he even found it "ridiculous and vacuous."

On July 10, 1915, James wrote a long letter to Wells expressing in detail his view of the matter. After commenting on Wells's failure to perceive the truth of James's view of things, the letter continued, "Of course for myself I live, live intensely and am fed by life, and my value, whatever it be, is in my own kind of expression of that." The fact that James's novels provided an experience utterly strange to Wells seemed, to the former, all the more reason why Wells should read them. James emphasized that it was when "history and curiosity have been determined in the way most different from my own that I want to get at them—precisely *for* the extension of life, which is the novel's best gift." The attitude toward the novel which James manifests here was one he held throughout his maturity.

Almost a quarter of a century earlier he had written an appreciative introduction to Kipling's *Soldiers Three,* a work that embodies experience certainly foreign to Henry James. Still, he took the opportunity to encourage critics to welcome such departures from familiar literary fare. James identified himself with a critic "who has, *a priori,* no rule for a literary production but that it shall have genuine life." Such a critic, he added, likes a writer "exactly in proportion as he is a challenge, an appeal to interpretation," to the extent, in short, that he made demands upon the critic's thought and feeling.

James's view of the intimate relationship that should exist between the artist and his product made it imperative that the artist be free to select his own material. The choice of subject should not be open to criticism, since it was more or less thrust upon him by life. His freedom was in reality a freedom from external pressures, any "thou-shalt-nots" applied by society. It is with the artist's *use* of the subject (as subject matter) that the reader and critic are concerned, and on this ground the artist might be held entirely responsible. "His treatment of it . . . is what he actively gives; and it is with what he gives that we are critically concerned." James did feel that the artist was obliged to seek out what had interested him most in his subject and to present it in such a way that it would interest the reader. The ways of being interesting were, of course, "as various as the temperament of man, and they are successful in proportion as they reveal a particular mind, different from others."

James held that there were just as many kinds of fiction as there were writers, since each writer had to deal with his own experience as he saw best. Each writer was obliged only to have a thorough perception of his subject, to see the way that presented most of it, and to be consistent in expressing it that way. While this view of the matter might seem all-embracing, it is actually very strict. It condemns the great body of writers who establish no felt relation with their subject but pour bucketfuls of formula onto the mass market; it excludes writers who pad and disguise their subject with irrelevant details, description, characters, scenes, and so forth; it eliminates writers who warp their subject matter to fit happy or unhappy endings, to shock or edify their readers, or simply to exploit their own personality.

If a writer did cultivate his personal sense of things, expressed what he most deeply thought and felt about his subject, the result was a highly personal style. This, as often as not, brought him into critical disrepute, as James well knew. In the course of his writing career his style had undergone considerable change, but it was always distinctive, even at the beginning. He continuously experimented with stylistic devices that he thought might aid his expression. He dealt with unusual and difficult material. In each case he tried to express his personal sense of the matter, and throughout his career he had to cope with the criticism of friend and foe because of the very qualities that were most his own.

To his brother William's repeated exhortation that he write a novel in a clear, direct style, avoiding his customary manner, James replied with weary resignation, that his brother seemed condemned to look at his work from "a point of view remotely alien to mine in writing it, and to the conditions out of which, *as* mine, it has inevitably sprung . . ." What was needed was for William to make the effort to see the material from his brother's point of view, to set aside presuppositions about subject and form, about the novel itself, and simply give himself over as fully as possible to the process of feeling and understanding what his brother's work had to offer. James realized that it was difficult for a reader to acquire his viewpoint and that he was often alone in what he considered to be the interest of a subject. Nevertheless he remained firm in his conviction that an artist must proceed according to what interests him most in his subject. Artists had to be taken "absolutely and utterly" on their own conditions, not on what they might give.

The novelist and friend of James, Paul Bourget, had suffered at the hands of critics because of his unusual style, and in the course of a letter discussing Bourget's work James remarked that each worthwhile artist must be aware that certain aspects of his work appeared to be deformities. This was inevitable when one tried to give one's personal sense of things. He wrote, "Each of us, from the moment we are worth our salt, writes as he can and only as he can, and his writing at all is conditioned upon the very things that from the standpoint of another method most lend themselves to criticism. And we each know much better than anyone else can what the defect of our inevitable form may appear . . . probably, I really understand better than anyone except yourself why, to do the thing at all, you must use your own, and nobody's else, trick of presentation. No two men in the world have the same idea, image and measure of presentation." This was a dedicated artist writing, and the phrase "as he can" did not refer to any easy, spontaneous overflowing, but to the result of an honest and exhaustive consideration of the subject and to expression guided by the utmost craftsmanship. With this view in mind, such terms as "the well-made novel" and "the art of the novel" must be used with caution. They tend to suggest that there is one kind of novel that is well made, or certain techniques essentially connected with the novel as an art-form. This is a false emphasis. James contended that a novelist was successful when he grasped the fullest significance of his subject and when he was able to express successfully what had chiefly interested him in it. What was vital was the novelist's personal sense of the matter; questions of technique were secondary, and the accolade "well made" an *ex post facto* consideration.

There is a passage in *A Small Boy and Others* that deals with James's glimpes of what he called "the old order" of French drama. This was an order which depended upon the resources of the actor and actress almost exclusively, and in which the material resources of the drama—settings, costumes, and the rest—were counted almost as nonessentials. The play, itself, was secondary to one thing. "That one thing was the quality, to say nothing of the quantity, of the actor's personal resource, technical history, tested temper, proved experience; on which almost everything had to depend . . ." In surveying the evolution of the theater since the day of "the old order," it seemed to James that the situation had become reversed. There, as elsewhere in the arts, the personal equation had been reduced to a contribution of "the loosest and sparest," while mechanical conditions, things not really of the essence, had taken over the burden. James had experimented elaborately in trying to find ways and means of more fully expressing what he wanted to say in his art. There are periods in his work when the technique heavily overburdens the substance. But in his major phase the enormous apparatus subserves beautifully the act of personal expression. It is one of the minor tragedies of literary history that critics in the generations succeeding James have been so quick to snap up his technical apparatus and so slow to do that without which a knowledge of the apparatus is beside the point, namely, to do their best to feel and understand and deeply experience a work of art, to appreciate what the unique quality is of each artist's window upon the world, before proceeding to their critical evaluations.

The personal equation that had characterized the drama of the French theatre in the day of "the old order," and which so appealed to James, was an exhibition of the same personal quality he sought for the novel. Here, too, he found most desirable the individual performance, the unique elements of each artist's expression, the absence of extrinsic machinery. For this reason he especially objected to illustrations and scorned the new fashion of relying upon statistics, photographs, "science," the tendency towards a stereotyped and journalistic prose, the selection of subject matter not from personal experience but from an array calculated to tempt the public appetite, and all other forces that were depersonalizing the art of fiction and making it a mass product for mass consumption.

Few writers, it is true, had James's dedication to art. James observed that far from being the rule, a cultivated, personal style was the exception, and even an exception for which an apology seemed to be thought necessary. The prevalent state of the novel suggested to James the image of each writer as a mill,

grinding "with regularity and with a certain commercial fineness" an article for which there was at least a comfortable
demand. There was little that savoured of personal experience
in this process, except as certain mills were associated with certain specialities providing a "useful, well-tested prescription."

A personal style is a rare thing, James recognized, and as a
result many people could not be expected to understand it.
They would object to style as something affected and confusing.
Yet, he felt the artist should strive to develop his own treatment
of material, his own "rendering of the text," and trust that some
kind of public would eventually come to appreciate it. The
usual charge is that such a style is "affected," and in one sense
of the term, James wholeheartedly agreed, but not in the sense
that implies falsity and insincerity. On the contrary, the artist's
expression is all the more genuine for his effort to manipulate
the prose medium in such a way as to capture the subtleties and
complexities that characterize his view of the subject. His search
for the right phrase, the proper tone and emphasis is guided by
his positive care for the interest of his subject and its organic
development, not by any desire to attract attention through an
artful juggling of words and phrases. James's final word on the
matter may be taken as that he put on the lips of Gabriel Nash,
in *The Tragic Muse,* when Nick Dormer asked him if his writing was not "a trifle affected." Nash replied, " 'That's always the
charge against a personal manner: if you've any at all people
think you've too much. Perhaps, perhaps—who can say? The
lurking unexpressed is infinite, and affectation must have
begun, long ago, with the first act of reflective expression—the
substitution of the few placed articulate words for the cry or
the thump or the hug. Of course one isn't perfect; but that's the
delightful thing about art, that there's always more to learn

and more to do; it grows bigger the more one uses it and meets more questions the more they come up. No doubt I'm rough still, but I'm in the right direction: I make it my business to testify for the fine.' "

10

Art is art in every country, and the novel . . . is the novel in every tongue, and hard enough work they have to live up to that privilege without our adding another muddle to the problem. James, Collaboration *(1893).*

Art and Society

HENRY JAMES DESCRIBED HIS WRITING OF FICTION AS AN "ACT OF life," and this term suggests the important truth that the creative process is not only continuous with everyday experience, but is a particularly meaningful and deeply felt kind of experience, with roots that extend far out into society, both present and past. Art, he insisted, should multiply our relations with life, and he believed artists must draw their inspiration from their experience. Clearly, if art was to be vital, it had to respond to the forces that were actively shaping contemporary culture. More than most members of society, the artist was apt to arrive at a clear perception of his experience by the very fact of having to work it out as a subject. Through his art, he could clarify for others what was happening in the social order. Partly for this reason, James expressed material that promised to comment meaningfully upon the social conditions of his day, such as the conflict between European and American standards, or the conflict arising within the individual consciousness as the result of shifting social ideas.

James's letters and other personal writings after the turn of the century disclose an increased concern on his part with the importance and potentiality of the individual human being. Anticipating the choice that was to confront dramatically many of the artists who would succeed him, he expressed himself strongly in favor of those modes of behavior which would preserve personal integrity as against those which would blend the

146

individual into the mass. He vigorously opposed any static organization of theories about art, as well as the pressures that sought to make taste and ideas in general conform to a norm. He wanted each individual to cultivate his own sense of things and to realize to the full his capacity for growth. There is a humanistic principle at the root of James's endeavor. The careful analysis of experience he so urgently advised was intended to discover the worthwhile values operative in contemporary culture. It was supposed to rescue precious elements in tradition and manners, and to preserve the essentials of human dignity from the tremendous pressures of change, materialism, and naturalism that threatened to engulf the age.

Although he had a strong desire to keep his personal life private, James provided the public with a more nearly complete record of the genesis and growth of his work than has any other novelist, and he supplemented this with many discussions of the art of the novel. He felt keenly an obligation to instruct both artists and the public in order that art might not only become better in itself, but thereby become a more effective instrument for social improvement. It is necessary to note, however, that James believed art served society best when the artist did the best work of which he was capable, and each artist had to determine that matter for himself. The last thing James had in mind was that society should determine what the artist should do. Of course, society would always try to impose its conditions upon the artist, but for the artist to heed such conditions was to run the risk of degrading both himself and society.

The relationship between the artist and society, as James saw it in practice over a long span of years, was characterized more by antagonism than by any recognition of mutual need and responsibility. On its side, society chose to look to art for non-aesthetic functions—chiefly education and amusement—and even these were interpreted narrowly. The artist, by and large, held out as little to society. There was a retreat from common, shared experience to unrelated individual and subjective worlds. It was the era of the ivory tower, of the "aristocratic and esoteric," and other withdrawals reflecting a lack of common purpose, of unifying beliefs and ideals. In the face of this separation, James ceaselessly waged a battle to restore the artist to his place as a responsible cultural leader while preserving, at the same time, the highest standards for art.

James recognized that there was considerable worth attached to the incidental contributions art could make to society. But its greatest value for society was that it could offer aesthetic experience of a kind more meaningful to the mind and spirit of man than all but a very few experiences encountered in the usual lifetime. While he deplored efforts to turn the novel into a vehicle for teaching, James pointed out that aesthetic experience could be more effective than any explicit teaching as an instrument for cultural improvement. Aesthetic experience, while directing no more imperatives to the reader, could reveal a possible ideal and make the public aware of what could be and hence critical of what is.

When James was doing some of his finest work, the naturalistic novel was in full stride in France and was rapidly attracting devotees in England and America. James urged writers devoted to naturalism not to neglect the nobler aspects of their experience, especially their moral reaction to evil and ugliness; he pointed out the advantages, not merely to art but to society, of showing "the opposite side of the coin." By appealing to the imagination, he argued, the artist can work on those elements in the public mind which activate moral good. By opposing the evil and ugly with a counterpart of the good and the beautiful in aesthetic experience, the artist could communicate a felt awareness of what the better condition might be. This is not didacticism at all; it conducts no campaign for local and temporary moral values, and, in fact, the artist is not primarily concerned with communicating any ideas at all. James's intention was of a far more general nature. He hoped, by involving his public in an aesthetic experience that was both morally significant and convincingly real, to lead men to examine and readjust their own values.

James always exercised a keen discrimination in morals and in art, and his struggle to satisfy his own principles in these matters and yet not altogether lose his public was one which knew no ending. His determination to write as tastefully as he knew how was put to the test early in his literary career. By the year 1872, when his letters from Europe to the *Nation* met with adverse public criticism, James was forced to make a decision about submitting to the public taste. He deferred to the opinions of his brother, William, and W. D. Howells on the over-refinement of his writing, but stipulated that beyond a certain point he would not go. In a letter to William (September 22 and 28, 1872), he described himself as a writer "who must give up the ambition of ever being a free-going and light-paced enough writer to please the multitude." He also remarked that more and more he was convinced that the public had no taste that a thinking man was bound to defer to. A short while after this, James was to lose his position with the *New York Tribune* because he would not alter his literary style to suit the newspaper's public. The usual objections to his work were that it was not "gossipy" enough, that it took too elevated a tone and dealt with material too refined for popular taste.

Twenty years later, in 1895, the same unhappy situation still existed, and James speculated in a notebook upon an idea for a story that would deal with a gifted artist who spent all his life trying "to take the measure of the huge, flat foot of the public." This idea reached story form as *The Next Time* (1895), which James included with *The Death of the Lion* (1894) and *The Coxon Fund* (1894) in one volume of the "New York Edition" of his work. As he observed in the preface to this volume, these three works all deal with the literary life and with "some noted adventure, some felt embarrassment, some extreme predicament, of the artist enamoured of perfection, ridden by his idea or paying for his sincerity." They offer an ironic commentary upon the relation of the serious artist to society. As a protest against the vulgar and stupid, against artistic compromise and as a criticism of social standards, they constitute an effective illustration of what James called "a civic use of the imagination."

The Death of the Lion is severe in its treatment of writers who seek primarily to achieve popularity, who have no serious concern for the quality of their work and do not base it upon genuine experience. "Dora Forbes" and "Guy Walsingham" illustrate the complete separation of such artists from their product. The former, it develops, is a man, and the latter, a woman. Another character, Mr. Morrow, typifies the publisher who has only the most superficial appreciation of art and criticism. Although he represents a syndicate of thirty-seven influential journals, he prefers the light, trivial and familiar to any serious literary work. Such artists and publishers in reality betrayed the public they pretended to serve.

The narrator of *The Next Time* speaks at one point of Ralph Limbert's idea of success. " 'He used to quote at me as a definition something from a nameless page of my own, some stray dictum to the effect that the man of his craft had achieved it when of a beautiful subject his expression was complete.' " James had already expressed a closely related idea in *The Les-*

son of the Master (1888), where St. George, a best-selling novelist, counsels Paul Obert to forego any · expectation of contemporary success, financial or critical, and to devote himself to his art.

When pressed to name the actual writers who were represented by such dedicated artists as Neil Paraday, Ralph Limbert, and Hugh Vereker, James replied that he could not do so, that they had been drawn from the resources of his own mind. Actually this was not entirely the case, as his correspondence with young writers indicates. Still, James considered it no personal embarrassment that he should produce no names. Rather, he considered it a public shame that there should be no evident examples of reaction against the general stupidity, vulgarity, and hypocrisy that abounded. To invent a splendid example of reaction was positively a public service. James called it "operative irony," since the portrayal in fine aesthetic terms of a sincere, gifted artist was an effort to correct the abuse of literature. It offered a lucid example of what might be, as well as what was the case. "How can one consent to make a picture of the preponderant futilities and vulgarities and miseries of life," James asked, "without the impulse to exhibit as well from time to time, in its place, some fine example of the reaction, the opposition or the escape?" In his own experience and in that of many of his friends, James found abundant material for such a fine example.

James had to learn very early how to cope with the public. He had to ignore the popular cry or give up his own way of writing altogether. Even so, he still suffered occasionally from the public's attitude. When he lapsed into obscurity after the bright success of *Daisy Miller* (1878), he was dismayed, and the failure of *Guy Domville* on opening night, January 5, 1895, brought him sharp despair. But he quickly recovered from these blows and generally proved immune to the animadversions of reviewers and the public's disregard. Shortly after the publication of *The Tragic Muse* (1890), James received a letter from his brother William sparkling with praise and encouragement. William noted, however, that the work would appeal to a small, if select, company. James replied making plain the fact that he had no illusions about the book and "least of all about its circulation and 'popularity.' " He reasserted his freedom from such cares and his belief that an artist should dedicate himself to his work, have faith in his own sense of values, rather than heed a public, "the draggling after which simply leads one in the gutter." This same independence is repeated in a letter to Howells, who called James's attention to favorable American notices of *The Wings of the Dove* (1902). "American 'notices,' heaven save the mark!" James exclaimed, and added "my work definitely insists upon being independent of such phantasms and on unfolding itself wholly from its own 'innards.' "

The attitude of the Victorian public and publishers on the subject of sex was of special annoyance to James. The censorship they exercised seemed to him part of the conspiracy of prudery operating to obstruct any effort by English novelists to deal adequately with life. To the question, "Is it proper?" James said the proper rejoinder was, " 'Proper to what?' There is only one propriety the painter of life can ask of his morsel of material: Is it, or is it not, of the stuff of life?" One of James's earliest experiences with editorial censorship occurred in 1873, in connection with the publication of *The Madonna of the Future* by the *Atlantic*. Howells had approved the story but recommended the excision of one episode as "risky for the magazine." Henry James, Sr. assumed responsibility for the cut. When James was told of the action, he wrote to his father expressing his regret and his "artistic" disapproval. "With such a standard of propriety," he declared, "it makes it a bad look-out ahead for imaginative writing. For what class of minds is it that such very timorous scruples are thought necessary?"

The great gift of the novel was an extension of life; it could achieve a sensuous surface that would appeal to the reader's feelings, and he could feel himself caught up in its dramatic oppositions; it could involve him in rich, complex experiences that were far more illuminating than those that composed his daily round. But to realize this possibility on any large scale there had to be mutual trust and respect on the part of both artist and public. As it was, the great conspiracy on the part of society to pretend certain areas of experience didn't exist made for distrust and contempt on both sides. The title character of *Greville Fane* (1893) was highly representative of the day's writers in that she was a kind of desperate literary drudge, who ". . . considered that she grovelled before the Rhadamanthus of the English literary tribunal, the celebrated and awful Young Person." And in his acid characterization of an editor, Mr. Beston of "The Cynosure" in *John Delavoy* (1898), James gives us a glimpse of the kind of publisher with whom writers had to contend. This editor revealed the rarest kind of intellectual economy, that of knowing nothing and valuing nothing save what would "do" for "The Cynosure." With "the question of sex in any degree," his magazine would have nothing whatever to do. The ironic touch James was aiming for here was the editor's conception of his public, "its ineffable sneakingness and baseness."

It is no wonder that so many artists capitulated to the public's tastes, or formed small mutual-admiration coteries, or denied their experience and cultivated the realm of phantasy. There was no denying the public's hypocrisy. James did not feel that every story involving sex or scandal was suitable for publication; he saw that the question was a complicated one. Yet he did feel that a decision on this matter was not successfully arrived at by arbitrarily excluding all stories involving such subject matter or censoring them. Above all the matter was not settled by trying to ignore fundamental elements in human experience. In his study of D'Annunzio's work James observes that most of the stories center about sex and that they are essentially vulgar. They were vulgar not because of this emphasis upon sexual matters, but because it was unattended by any general meaning. The action presented had little to discriminate it from an instinctive animal function. For all its presentation of actuality, there was no moral realism in D'Annunzio's work. So far as the significance of the passion he presented was concerned, he might as well have been the artisan of *The Madonna of the Future* (1873) crying, "Cats and monkeys—monkeys and cats—all human life is there!"

James also made a distinction between what attempted to cope seriously with human experience and what was simply trivial gossip. A reporter in *The Reverberator* (1888) learns all the secrets of an aristocratic French family and publishes them in an American newspaper. Such information sold newspapers, but the family was outraged and disgraced. Its members could not understand why anyone, let alone the American public, should be interested in their personal affairs. They considered it the vilest taste to pry into such a subject, particularly since the published facts, isolated from the context of family history, amounted to malicious half-truths. Peter Baron, a character in *Sir Dominick Ferrand* (1893), further illustrates James's position. Baron has his story declined, although presumably it is of merit, because it might cause a small scandal. Yet the publisher was anxious to obtain the letters of Sir Dominick Ferrand, which Baron had accidentally discovered, because of the sensation they would make. When Peter Baron asked that his story be published, this conversation ensued:

" 'Think of the scandal, Mr. Baron.'

'But isn't this other scandal just what you're going in for?'

'It will be a great public service.'

'You mean it will be a big scandal, whereas my poor story would be a very small one, and that it's only out of a big one that money's to be made.' "

In these and similar stories, James called attention to the cheap hypocrisy of the public attitude. He tried to place the bridge between the artist and public on a sounder moral foundation. As things stood, both were losers, and instead of shedding light on human problems, literature only added to the darkness.

At the heart of the matter was the ignorant, provincial, self-destroying attitude that refused to recognize the importance of art. This was what James dwelt upon in *The Tragic Muse* (1890). To demonstrate the importance he attached to art, James had one of the characters, Nick Dormer, sacrifice a political career that might have led to the prime-ministership in order to devote himself to art. James recognized in planning this that it would be regarded as improbable by the English public, since to ask them to accept somebody's willingness to pass up a useful profession for the sake of art was the same as to ask them to accept "somebody's willingness to pass mainly for an ass." Another character, Miriam Rooth, refused to give up her career as an artist to become the wife of a promising diplomat. By dramatizing these choices, James implied that art could be more rewarding, to both the artist and the community, than political and social success.

A good deal of James's irony in this novel is reserved for the popular attitude that art did not deserve the effort of serious study. Art was considered socially acceptable, when practised by amateurs, only when it was bad; it was something to be done at odd hours and for amusement only, "like a game of tennis or whist." Whenever anyone took art seriously, he was considered somehow to be criminally negligent. To devote oneself completely to art, carrying it as far as possible, was considered a kind of madness. This view of things was, to James, immoral not only because of its disservice to art, but because of its disservice to the community. While the public professed to be interested, above all else, in culture, it operated in actual fact to vitiate the greatest force for cultural advancement.

At the time when James wrote *The Tragic Muse,* English life was encumbered by an unusually elaborate apparatus of prohibitions. James's belief that "the whole thinking man is one" was opposed by a cultural milieu in which a man subscribed to different and often conflicting social values when he was engaged in his business, his religion, his amusement, and so forth. Although broad, revolutionary social movements were well under way (James dealt with one such movement in *The Princess Casamassima),* there was a mass desire for surface conformity and a veneration of "respectability." By their very nature, these conditions not only retarded what James called "the necessity of the mind, its simple necessity of feeling," but actively suppressed a free operation of personal taste and aesthetic expression.

For better or for worse, the art that was produced insisted upon reflecting the nature of the community that produced it. At the mid-century, when many artists sought inspiration in the work of another age, their expression became an artificial process. They did not respond to the conditions that had produced the work of the earlier periods which they chose to imitate, nor did they recognize any similarity between the conditions of the earlier periods and those of their own day. As a result, Tennyson produced emasculate Arthurian idylls and the Pre-Raphaelite painters their largely weak and sallow efforts. James satirized the Pre-Raphaelite painters as Mark Ambient's sister in *The Author of Beltraffio* (1884), "a restless romantic disappointed spinster, consumed with the love of Michael-Angelesque attitudes and mystical robes." It would seem probable, from a letter written to Alice James in 1869, that the character was first suggested by William Morris's wife, who once appeared before James in similar robes and attitudes. During the last quarter of the century, the great body of English literature and painting reflected weak aesthetic perceptions, warped experience, and an excessive concern with non-aesthetic material.

Many artists welcomed the artificial restraints of the Victorian decline as offering an excuse for not coping with their environment. Most of the "Decadents" and writers whose natural predilection was for romance took this excuse. The work of such men was usually too frothy to appeal to James's taste. He had become much too conscious of the public for which it had been designed and of the shallow material out of which it had been pieced together. Again and again, the work reflected the public taste, was a criticism of that taste, and if it expressed anything expressed the wish to escape or at best to play with the surface of life. As James indicated, there were exceptions to this; Conrad and Stevenson, for example, were true artists, and James praised the fine quality of numerous individual works. And despite all of his animadversions on conditions of English life during the last quarter of the century, it provided him with much of his most precious material; in fact, the difficult position of art and the artist proved one of his richest veins.

Most precious to James was the capacity of art to bring an

individual an aesthetic awareness of societies far removed from
him by time or space. The way in which a work of art could
evoke a sharp sense of the public for which it had been made
and of the conditions out of which it had grown occurred to
James in reading William Wetmore Story's account of a generation that seemed to have too swiftly receded into the past. James
had spoken many times of art's capacity to transmit a sense of
the past and of the importance of such a capacity to society.
Perhaps art's chief historical value in this respect is that it can
recapture the past in terms of a unified perception. It does not
artificially abstract an idea, isolate a custom, analyze an event.
James did not consider such questions as the degree to which
the observer might be aware that he is dealing with history, or
to what extent a knowledge of the actual historical conditions
connected with the work of art is necessary, or whether the work
of art might be only a reiteration of conventionalized art forms,
and so forth. He did, however, in his discussions of Balzac,
George Sand, Hawthorne, and elsewhere testify to the power of
art, through its aesthetic qualities, to evoke for him a sharp
awareness of the past.

What interested him most in this relation with the past was
the awareness it brought him of human conditions—not so
much the actual physical conditions of life as the way people
felt, why they acted as they did, the whole moral pattern of
their lives. He enjoyed a sense of the place, but his interest centered on essentially human considerations. This basic interest
in the spirit of man, as conveyed aesthetically rather than as
dismembered or abstracted in philosophy, led James to de-
nounce such artificial divisions as nationality in his effort to
make society aware of the great body of human experience that
could be shared through art.

Above all it struck him as silliness to think of art as the product of any one country or as differing from one country to the next. The experience with which art deals might vary, but art itself was the common property of the human race. James's short story *Collaboration* (1893) concerns a German pianist and a French poet who admire each other's work and decide to collaborate on an opera. This action estranges the poet's fiancée and her mother because of their antipathy to Germans. They are incapable of enjoying any work by a German artist. An American becomes angry with the German when the latter fails to appreciate an English poetess and the "American novel." The whole muddle is supposed to illustrate that national designations are merely artificial terms designed to aid cataloguers, reviewers, and tradesmen and represent preoccupations "utterly foreign" to the work of art.

Throughout his long career, James had been concerned intimately with the international scene, and as his career drew to a close he saw in the "achieved social fusion" which then existed and was to grow wider and denser a new field for the novelist. In the future, he believed, thematic material that went beyond the usual prejudices that attended a society divided up into many religious, racial, and national groups would appeal more successfully to the imagination. In short, James recognized that the battles raging in the heart of man were not of this time, of that place, but were enduring and universal. Every artist who penetrated that battlefield went alone and without identifying banners, and although the warring forces might bear temporary names, they were as old as man himself. There was a public, too, that saw easily across all the artificial barriers in the human community. It was a small public, but a growing one, and James was encouraged sufficiently by his knowledge of it to hope for "some eventual sublime consensus of the educated."

In promoting "the dauntless fusions to come," the aesthetic

experience afforded by art was to play a major role. It enabled a man to live beyond his time and place, to penetrate to that rarely accessible peak, another man's mind and, briefly, to live there. The ability to make this possible was the artist's great gift to society. Meanwhile, for the artist himself, there was the work of seeing and doing, the act of possessing himself of as much as possible of what happened to him. At the maturity of his career, when he turned to look back over the long road he had traveled, James decided that what lived longest in his vision was not the value of art to this one or that one, nor even so questionable a thing as success. What he most treasured was the wondrous experience of the creative process itself, "the inveterate romance of the labour." In the summer of 1891, when he paused to consider all he had seen, felt, and achieved, he resolved that for the future he would "strike as many notes, deep, full and rapid," as he could. He resolved to "try everything, do everything, render everything—be an artist, be distinguished, to the last." In carrying out this resolve he demonstrated how vast and solid a bond could be forged between the artist and society.

The next twenty-odd years brought an astonishing amount of production, with continued freshness, spontaneity and artistic development. When James had less than a year to live, he received a letter from Henry Adams bewailing the emptiness of life. James asserted in his reply that he had still as many reactions as possible in the presence of life and sent along a book as proof of it. "It's, I suppose, because I am that queer monster, the artist," he mused, "an obstinate finality, an inexhaustible sensibility. . . . Hence the reactions—appearance, memories, many things, go on playing upon it with consequences that I note and 'enjoy' (Grim word!) noting. It all takes doing—and I do. I believe I shall do yet again—it is still an act of life."

Notes

The numerals at the left refer to page and then to line in this book. The two italicized words which follow the numerals are the end of the quotation or phrase which is being annotated. In the notes the following abbreviations have been used:

AN *The Art of the Novel,* Critical Prefaces by Henry James, N. Y. and London, 1947.
EL Henry James, *Essays in London and Elsewhere,* N. Y., 1893.
FP Henry James, *French Poets and Novelists,* London, 1878.
NN Henry James, *Notes on Novelists with some Other Notes,* N. Y., 1914.
NR Henry James, *Notes and Reviews,* Cambridge, Mass., 1921.
PP Henry James, *Partial Portraits,* N. Y., 1888.
VR Henry James, *Views and Reviews,* Boston, 1908.

In references to the works listed above, the date of an article's original publication is supplied when considered pertinent. Unless otherwise noted, references to James's fiction are from *The Novels and Tales of Henry James,* The New York Edition, 26 vols., 1907–17.

CHAPTER 1

14, 2 *of life."* Henry James, *The Middle Years,* N. Y., 1917, p. 11.
15, 4 *I stood,"* Henry James, *Notes of a Son and Brother,* N. Y., 1914, p. 306.
15, 5 *Russell Lowell,* January, 1892. EL, 48–49.
16, 5 *on fiction.* Review of Nassau W. Senior's *Essays on Fiction, North American Review,* October, 1864.
16, 10 *of life"* Notes of a Son and Brother, 64.

17, 14   *grasping imagination," The Letters of Henry James,* Selected
         and Edited by Percy Lubbock, 2 vols., N. Y., 1920, I, 30 (January
         16, 1871).
17, 25   *a master." Ibid.*
19, 20   *the interest,"* F. O. Matthiessen, *The James Family,* N. Y., 1947,
         p. 485. Quoted from a letter, Henry James to Robert S. Rantoul,
         June, 1904.
19, 28   *English novelists,* Review of William Dean Howells' *A Foregone
         Conclusion, Nation,* January 7, 1875.
20, 12   *their immorality.* September 14, 1865. NR, 78–79.
21, 6   *him intellectually." Letters,* I, 46.
21, 30   *historical truth. Nation,* August 15, 1876, 126.
22, 6   *high-life,"* December, 1875. FP, 144.
22, 11   *of Balzac.* 1902. NN, 132.
22, 17   *shown before.* June 19, 1913. NN, 146.
22, 25   *cultivated consciousness."* NN, 156–57.
23, 13   *an absurdity.* FP, 256–57.
23, 27   *for Flaubert.* January, 1884. PP, 319.
24, 1   *his barriers."* March, 1893. EL, 149.
25, 3   *the soul."* EL, 150.
25, 16   *sexual impulse.* March, 1888. PP, 258.
25, 31   *us today."* May, 1888. EL, 154.
26, 29   *Parisian scene.* August, 1883. PP, 214–15.
28, 4   *it not."* September, 1884. PP, 393.
28, 7   *by imitation."* August, 1903. NN, 60.
28, 23   *an artifice."* NN, 47.
29, 30   *by themselves. Notes of a Son and Brother,* 25–27.

CHAPTER 2

31, 11   *dynamic nature.* PP, 388–89.
33, 17   *to offer. Notes of a Son and Brother,* 169.
35, 16   *but "nasty."* April 27, 1876. FP, 78.
36, 4   *of subject-matter.* 1891. VR, 233–34.
36, 19   *to him.* April, 1866. NR.
37, 12   *moral beauty."* October 11, 1866. NR, 225–26.
39, 18   *not philosophic,"* July, 1877. FP, 204.
40, 6   *more unions."* January, 1897. NN, 185–86.
40, 10   *and improving.* NN, 179.
41, 8   *the soul."* April, 1914. NN, 228.
41, 17   *philosophical novelist. Vide, Nation,* August 16, 1866. Also, VR,
         "The Novels of George Eliot," (October, 1866).

42, 4   *idealizing reflection.* December, 1876. PP, 71–72. Also, October, 1868. VR, 136.
43, 3   *George Eliot.* May, 1885. PP, "The Life of George Eliot."
44, 4   *ascetic passion. . . ."* April, 1874. FP, 279.
44, 11 *morally interesting."* FP, 277.
44, 23 *of joy."* FP, 318.
45, 19 *accompany him."* PP, 300.
46, 12 *perpetual refreshment."* PP, 296–97.
46, 22 *new writers Vide,* "The New Novel," NN, especially 325–26.
48, 2   *post-office.'* " *A Bundle of Letters,* XIV, 497.
48, 25 *well somewhere. . . .'* " *Ibid.,* 498.
48, 29 *with life."* Benvolio, XXIV, 309.
49, 8   *it out."* The James Family, 300 (letter, William James to Henry James, Jr., January 9, 1883).
49, 12 *of it."* Ibid., 301.

CHAPTER 3

53, 17 *Whitman's Drum-taps.* November 16, 1865. VR.
53, 18 *Mild-mannered Trollope Vide.* NR, reviews of *Lindisfarn Chase, Miss Mackenzie, Can You Forgive Her?,* and *The Belton Estate.*
53, 21 *his author."* October 12, 1865. NR, 102.
54, 5   *their reason.* January, 1865. NR, 44.
55, 16 *for success."* VR, 87.
56, 2   *these men.* NR, "A French Critic."
56, 24 *in hand."* A review of Sainte-Beuve's "Portraits," *Nation,* June 4, 1868, formerly attributed to James but now considered to be by his father, takes the same position on Sainte-Beuve, ". . . that he is very little of a moralist and, in a really liberal sense of the word, not overmuch of a thinker."
56, 26 *"Literary Studies,"* Nation, April 6, 1876.
57, 14 *for life."* Review of "Correspondance de C. A. Sainte-Beuve," *North American Review,* January, 1880.
58, 9   *way round."* EL, 264–65.
59, 3   *her associations.* February 22, 1866. NR, 154–55.
59, 9   *Hugo's heart.* April 12, 1866. NR, 199.
60, 1   *the novelist."* July, 1883. PP, 97.
60, 8   *measurable meanings."* PP, 101.
60, 14 *good ear."* PP, 105.
60, 32 *they shed."* April, 1888. PP, 144.
61, 7   *comparatively denied."* 1914. NN, 235.
62, 1   *strongest feeling.* 1897. NN, 167.

62, 25 *their 'expansion.'* " July, 1877. FP, 220.
63, 12 *"general humanity."* 1914. NN, 224.

CHAPTER 4

64, 5 *demand expression. Op. cit.,* 24–25.
64, 24 *of creation."* The Notebooks of Henry James, eds. F. O. Matthiessen and Kenneth B. Murdock, N. Y., 1947, p. 318. *Vide,* also, pp. 92, 112, *et passim.*
65, 28 *of art."* Notebooks, 318.
65, 31 *a mine." Ibid.*
67, 6 *of humor." Op. cit.,* XIV, 258.
69, 5 *impelling force.* AN, 31.
71, 4 *developed reader."* Letters, I, 66, November 14, 1878.
71, 21 *at all.* Letters, I, 325.
72, 1 *richly responsible."* AN, 62.
73, 3 *its completest. . . ."* AN, 37.
73, 12 *general dishumanisation,"* AN, 244.
73, 18 *be aware," Ibid.*
74, 3 *it felt."* Henry James, *William Wetmore Story and His Friends,* 2 vols., London, 1903, I, 11–12.
74, 24 *and quiet.* AN, 27.
75, 4 *passionate sympathy."* Atlantic Monthly, "Taine's English Literature," April, 1872, pp. 469–70.
75, 20 *are there."* Notebooks, 135, August 30, 1893.
76, 5 *of joy." Op. cit.,* VII, 338.
76, 9 *for reflection.* NN, 130.
76, 12 *to develop.* NN, 337.
76, 31 *to date."* Letters, II, 181–82, March 3, 1911.
77, 2 *Singer Sargent.* Henry James, *Picture and Text,* N. Y., 1893, "John S. Sargent," p. 115.
77, 17 *a house."* Notebooks, 137, December 24, 1893. *Vide,* ed. note, 137–38.

CHAPTER 5

79, 9 *"intellectual nostril."* AN, 142.
79, 14 *and clearer." Ibid.*
79, 23 *actually "experienced." Vide, Mind,* 1884, IX, 1–26, "On some Omissions of Introspective Psychology," William James.
80, 13 *of method. Cf.* NN, 14–15.
82, 12 *not hang.* NN, 342.
82, 31 *and Dostoevsky.* Letters, II, 237–38 (to Hugh Walpole, May 19, 1912).

83, 8   *of form," Vide,* AN, 84, and NN, 328.
84, 3   *the material. . . ."* EL, 242.
84, 15 *different enough. William Wetmore Story,* II, 234–35.
84, 30 *interested him. Letters,* II, 234 (to Mrs. Humphrey Ward, July 26, 1899).
84, 32 *penetrable places";* AN, 277.
85, 15 *its meaning."* FP, 224.
86, 5   *dramatically, interesting." Letters,* II, 320–21 (to Mrs. Alfred Sutro, June 25, 1913).
87, 9   *the subject. . . ." Notebooks,* 102–03.
88, 1   *the 'story.' "* February 22, 1866. NR, 160.
88, 4   *and authority."* AN, 44.

CHAPTER 6

89, 23 *became 'scenes.' " Op. cit.,* 185–86.
92, 21 *architectural quality. Nona Vincent,* XXVI, 451–52.
93, 28 *will grow." Notebooks,* 268–69.
94, 17 *a part."* NN, 192.
95, 9   *of parts." William Wetmore Story,* I, 341.
95, 15 *of 'treatment.' "* Henry James, *The American Scene,* 1907, N. Y., 137–38.
96, 8   *and sharp."* AN, 14.
96, 30 *organic form."* AN, 84–85.
97, 8   *the whole. Vide.* PP, 92.
97, 22 *a harmony."* AN, 136.
98, 4   *work in." The Sense of the Past,* XXVI, 343.
98, 17 *monotonous hue." Lady Barberina,* XIV, 4.
99, 5   *the novel. Vide,* AN, 322–24.
99, 30 *the thread."* PP, 400.
100, 17 *cultivated credulity,"* AN, 171.
100, 27 *of foreshortening,"* AN, 234.
100, 31 *and condensations."* AN, 240.
101, 4 *general use." Ibid.*
101, 11 *were atmospheric."* AN, 153–54.
101, 22 *true one.* AN, 115–16.
101, 30 *for trigonometry."* NN, 90–91.
102, 5 *may dwell."* NN, 80.

CHAPTER 7

105, 16 *moral repose."* November 9, 1865. NR, 110.
108, 10 *splendid desperadoes."* AN, 258.
108, 17 *to us."* AN, 257.

109, 4   *of nature."* AN, 253.
110, 8   *the realities,"* AN, 149.
111, 24   *not, later." Notebooks,* 18.
112, 12   *are present.* NN, 279.
114, 1   *English mind."* Henry James, *England at War: an essay,* "The Question of the Mind," London, 1915, p. 12.
114, 21   *of it." Letters,* I, 72 (January 31, 1880).
114, 32   *in 1886. Harper's Weekly,* "William Dean Howells," June 19, 1886.
115, 27   *remains appreciable."* AN, 164.
117, 7   *pitying hand!' "* Henry James, *The Two Magics: The Turn of the Screw, Covering End,* N. Y., 1907. *Covering End,* 317.
117, 13   *of others.' " Ibid.,* 318.
117, 29   *be enough." The Sense of the Past,* 48–49.

CHAPTER 8

120, 18   *for thought." Notes of a Son and Brother,* 180–81.
120, 22   *form only. . . ." Ibid.,* 181.
121, 1   *to love. . . ."* PP, 24.
122, 23   *about Europe. A Small Boy and Others,* 283–85.
124, 13   *explosive principle."* AN, 278.
125, 1   *imaginative life."* NN, 315.
125, 20   *and "do."* NN, 106–07.
126, 13   *each attempt."* PP, 142.
126, 21   *his coat."* PP, 140.
128, 16   *to utterance." The Tragic Muse,* VII, 203.
128, 24   *its place." Ibid.,* 206.
129, 12   *the newspaper. . . ."* AN, 279–80.
129, 17   *of direction. Vide,* Henry James, *The Question of Our Speech,* Boston and N. Y., 1905, p. 11.
129, 20   *of speech. Ibid.,* 24.
131, 6   *aesthetic vision,"* AN, 346–47.

CHAPTER 9

135, 2   *to offer."* NN, 51–52.
136, 18   *into literature.* PP, 405–06.
136, 23   *whole field."* PP, 406.
137, 6   *the producer."* PP, 406.
137, 11   *with art.* NN, 422. *Vide,* also, Henry James, *Hawthorne,* London, 1879, p. 61.
137, 15   *moral meaning."* FP, 221.
138, 21   *is one. . . ."* FP, 64–65.

139, 3 *and vacuous." Letters,* II, 489–90, July 10, 1915.
139, 9 *of that." Ibid.*
139, 15 *best gift." Ibid.*
139, 23 *genuine life."* 1891. VR, 227–28.
140, 5 *critically concerned."* NN, 259–60.
140, 10 *from others."* PP, 384.
141, 9 *inevitably sprung. . . ." Letters,* II, 43–44, November 23, 1905.
141, 19 *and utterly." Ibid.,* I, 164–65 (to W. D. Howells, May 17, 1890), *Vide,* also, AN, 122.
142, 4 *of presentation." Letters,* I, 288–89, August 19, 1898.
142, 28 *to depend. . . ." James Family,* 238 (to William James, November 11, 1902).
142, 32 *and sparest," A Small Boy and Others,* 361–62.
144, 2 *commercial fineness."* PP, 142.
145, 4 *the fine." The Tragic Muse,* VII, 172–74.

CHAPTER 10

149, 22 *the multitude." James Family,* 320–21, September 22 and 28. 1872.
150, 1 *the public." Notebooks,* 180, January 26, 1895.
150, 9 *his sincerity."* AN, 221.
150, 14 *the imagination."* AN, 223.
150, 31 *was complete.' " The Next Time,* XV, 183.
151, 16 *operative irony,"* AN, 222.
151, 23 *the escape?"* AN, 223.
152, 8 *and 'popularity.' " Letters,* I, 170, July 23, 1890.
152, 17 *own 'innards.' " Ibid.,* I, 407, December, 1902.
152, 25 *of life?"* NN, 295.
153, 3 *thought necessary?" James Family,* 121–23, February 3, 1873.
153, 18 *Young Person." Greville Fane,* XVI, 123.
153, 27 *and baseness." Notebooks,* 245–46.
154, 7 *essentially vulgar.* NN, 292.
155, 8 *be made.' " Sir Dominick Ferrand,* XXVI, 434–35.
155, 26 *an ass."* AN, 83
156, 4 *or whist." The Tragic Muse,* VII, 18.
159, 14 *utterly foreign." Collaboration,* XXVII, 167.
159, 17 *social fusion."* AN, 202–03.
159, 31 *the educated."* AN, 203.
160, 13 *the labour."* AN, 287.
160, 18 *the last." Notebooks,* 106, July 13, 1891.
160, 32 *of life." Letters,* II, 361, March 21, 1914.

Index

169